PRAISE FOR T

I love this series. It is well wri ...ell
built fantasy world surrounding ...e one comes out I
immediately drop everything to read it. She ties in little tidbits
from her other books too, making for some fun easter eggs
to find!

Amelia has a true talent for putting together a story, and the
best of all is just how wonderfully HOT it all is together too.
It's no faint praise to say that this is simply one of the most
believable, enjoyable, and beautiful pairings I've ever read
about; it feels like seeing right into the lives and love of two
people.

I really enjoyed the writing; I thought it was crisp and vivid,
and really pulled the characters off the page

I am pleased to say that I thoroughly enjoyed reading this
story. It is definitely a new take on the usual shifter stories and
I loved the detail of the surroundings and the vulnerability of
the characters.

If you are new to Amelia's works, I'd definitely describe Amelia's books as not-just-another-fairytale, and she is able to write a very suspenseful action-packed novel, but somehow still focus on the romance at the same time. Its marvellous! If you are a fan of action/suspense movies, I'd definitely recommend you to give Amelia's works a go.

I went through the entire series, unable to stop reading, it was that good. The characters are real, they aren't some cookie-cutter fantasy. They seem deep and in-depth and like they could be actual people.

BLIND MAN'S WOLF

AMELIA FAULKNER

First electronic publication: December 2014.
First paperback publication: May 2018.
http://ameliafaulkner.com

Blind Man's Wolf is set in the UK, and as such uses British English throughout.

CONTENTS

GLOSSARY

Areet: All right. E.g. *Y'areet there, petal?* or *It's areet, in't it?*

Aye: Yes. *Aye, it was me.*

Barmpot: Fool. This tends to be used as a term of mild frustration or exasperation. It isn't too derogatory, but it's not all that fond either. *The fella's a total barmpot!*

Cadge: Borrow. *Can I cadge a tenner? I'll pay it back…*

Daft apeth: Fool. This is a term of fondness or endearment while still expressing how silly you think someone's being. *You don't have to pay me back ten quid, you daft apeth.*

Earwig: Eavesdrop. This can either be in, on, or as-is: *I was earwigging in on Albert t'other day* or *Oi, stop earwigging, it's rude!*

Gradely: Good. Excellent, even, especially combined with reet: *Aye, it were reet gradely!*

Happen: Reckon. *I'll 'appen as it'll take a few days.*

In't: In the or isn't it. *I'll be over in't morning* or *It in't time for dinner yet!*

Owt: Anything. *I didn't bring owt with me. Were I s'posed to?*

Reet: Right. Very. *I'll 'appen as it were reet gradely!*

Petal: Term of endearment. *Y'areet there petal?*

Tosser: Wanker. From 'tossing off', i.e. wanking. *Aye, 'e's a reet tosser, he is.*

Wazzock: Idiot. Mildly derogatory. *Then the wazzock dropped 'is trousers an' we all had a good laugh!*

ONE

Tiberius led Ellis astray again.

Ellis had left his gallery a little after midnight. It was well within normal for him to work so late: daytime wasn't an option and his assistant couldn't shoulder everything. While Ellis' grasp of the passage of time wasn't too precise, he was reasonably sure they had been out far longer than necessary.

"Stop," Ellis said.

Tiberius halted obediently.

Ellis slid his left sleeve up until he felt his watch. His fingers drifted across the flat dial and outer edge at once until he found both ball bearings.

Five to one.

At this time of year he still had at least five hours before sunrise, but every delay brought fear. What if tonight would be the night that Tiberius failed to get him home on time?

"Where are we?" he grumbled as he drew his sleeve down and returned to position. "Straight on, Tiberius."

Tiberius moved, and Ellis walked alongside him, straining to hear any clues as to their whereabouts.

Leaves crinkled underfoot as they continued. More leaves than on a pedestrian pavement, but there was a hard surface underfoot, so there were either more trees along this path than others, or it was maintained less frequently.

What vehicle traffic he could hear was distant. He wasn't alongside a road, or if he was it had nothing travelling along it. He couldn't detect any hints of the Tube, but the Tube stopped running around this time of night so that was no great help.

He bit his lip, then instructed the dog, "Turn left."

Tiberius adjusted course, and Ellis stepped onto softer ground.

"Stop." Ellis crouched and placed his right hand lightly against the wet grass. There were leaves, too, covered in leftover rain. He stood and patted his hand dry against his trouser leg, then reached for his glasses and slid them up his forehead. He peered around slowly, searching for any glimmer of light.

Before he had been turned, Ellis was utterly blind even in twilight. What little vision hadn't been stolen entirely during the day needed a lot of light. Now that he was dead... undead... whatever he wanted to call himself, his senses were sharper. If he was lucky he could potentially make out the headlights of a car coming straight for him so long as it was mere seconds away from impact.

Trying to see was a last-ditch effort, and proved about as worthless as Ellis had expected. He found dim, colourless spots in the sky which were probably street lamps, but that was all. He pushed his glasses back into place and the dark lenses cut out even that small reminder of what was lost.

The clues taken together seemed to indicate that Tiberius had taken him to a park, and his mental map of Mayfair unfurled as he tried to figure out which one. Berkeley Square Gardens were closed after dusk and didn't re-open until after sunrise. Grosvenor Square Gardens were even more restrictive, as were Mount Street Gardens. He should have noticed if they had crossed Park Lane, but Hyde Park closed at midnight anyway. Tiberius shouldn't be able to enter any of them after midnight except Green Park; they all had gates which were closed and locked after hours.

Were they in Green Park, then? That wouldn't be too bad. He fell still and listened again.

In the distance, a small rodent met its end, most likely to a fox. He waited, and heard a flutter of leathery wings high overhead and a rustle as tiny bats grabbed tree branches and came to rest.

Ellis swore, keeping his voice quiet. He had to have reached St. James' Park. How the hell had he not noticed crossing Piccadilly or

The Mall? How had they walked all the way through Green Park without him realising it? If he followed the path all the way to Buckingham Palace he may be able to attract a guard for assistance, but he figured that was likely one of the most densely-packed areas for CCTV cameras in their natural habitat. He'd be even deeper in poo if Her Majesty's Finest discovered a man who didn't show up on security screens.

"Turn around," he said. He twisted as Tiberius plodded around him, using his feet to be sure Tiberius had done a full 180 degrees. "Straight on. Good boy. Who's a good boy!"

They found the path within moments, turned right, and then Ellis had Tiberius find him a bench. He sat down and rewarded Tiberius with gentle fussing between his ears.

It was so strange. Tiberius would do all the right things. He was a damn good dog. They'd had their ups and downs after Ellis died, but things had seemed to be on the up again. Now they were getting lost, Tiberius would growl at strangers, and Ellis was forced to imagine what his existence would be like without his helper.

"Stay," he murmured, and dug into his coat pocket to drag out his mini braille display. 'Mini' was misleading: the device was about the size of a paperback book, and had cost him several hundred pounds. His dad wouldn't be too pleased about that, but Ellis wasn't in any position to care about what his dad thought these days. He popped the keyboard out of its case and rested it between his thighs.

He hadn't managed to master braille before he was turned. Ellis wasn't born blind: it crept up on him once he was an adult, so he'd never had to learn to replace sight with any other senses as a child. Once the knowledge had set in that his encroaching blindness was unavoidable, irreversible, he had tried, but his fingers couldn't differentiate between different configurations of small bumps. He visually learned the entire alphabet, but he couldn't read by touch.

Now that his senses had improved, he could feel the grain in a sheet of paper, let alone readily differentiate between individual dots in a cell. He couldn't help but be angry about that; if Jonas had turned him a couple of years earlier Ellis might even be able to see now, but no. Jonas had been as useless in his timing as he had with everything else.

Ellis grimaced. He didn't want to think about Jonas. Not right now.

Not ever.

He tapped the button combination to fire up the Bluetooth connectivity, and felt his phone buzz against his chest. Then it was a matter of patience. Ellis scrolled through his contacts list, fingers drifting from keys to the readout and back until he found Jay's number, then he pressed a text message out and sent it.

Jay, help. I think I'm in St. James' Park.

Ellis might be able to find his way back home from here, but if Jay were available it would save a lot of hassle.

He heard leaves crinkle. A heartbeat, calm, and drawing nearer. Footsteps.

Tiberius growled.

Ellis placed one hand over the reader and felt for Tiberius' harness with the other.

The person came closer, pace even until it halted. From the sound of breathing and heartbeat Ellis estimated the stranger to be no further than a metre away.

"Hey." It was a man's voice. It sounded friendly, curious, although perhaps a touch fearful too. "Is everything okay? Do you need any help?"

"I'm sorry." Ellis flashed a small smile. "He's not usually like this."

The stranger laughed a moment. It didn't sound too genuine. "What is he? Looks like an Alsatian, maybe?"

"German Shepherd, yeah. They tried me with a Labrador and we didn't get along too well. Tiberius, no."

Tiberius' growls subsided, but Ellis could still hear sounds emanating from him which expressed disapproval. Hopefully those sounds were below human hearing.

"I've never seen a German Shepherd guide dog before. I always thought it was, like you say, Labradors or Retrievers." The stranger chuckled again, still tense.

Ellis' phone buzzed, and he took his hand from the harness to read his text.

Wait there, it said. *I'll come get you.*

If Ellis breathed for anything other than talking, he would have exhaled with relief. As it was, he typed out and sent *Thank you. Tell Han I'm sorry*, and slid the keyboard back into its case.

"No," Ellis said while he returned the reader to his pocket. He tipped his head in the stranger's direction. "I've even heard of poodles. German Shepherds take training well, though. They love to work. I think it's just that the police snap most of them up." He gave a grin which he hoped suggested that Tiberius was a highly trained protector, and not a softie with wool between his ears. "But thanks, I'm fine. I'm waiting for a friend."

"If you want, I could wait with you?" the stranger offered.

"Oh, no, it's fine. He won't be long. Thank you. It's really kind of you." Ellis had long ago learned that the sighted were only trying to be helpful, even when their offers came across as a bit creepy.

"It's all good. I hope you haven't got to wait too long. Take care, okay?"

"You too. Thank you."

Tiberius' complaints subsided when the stranger's footsteps diminished into the distance, and Ellis fussed his head as he settled in to wait.

***

ELLIS SAT for twenty minutes before he heard new footsteps. These were hurried, and the owner's heartbeat was fast, his breathing heavy.

"Ellis," Jay panted. He skidded to a halt and placed his hand on Ellis' right shoulder. "Bloody hell, it's cold out. Are you okay?"

Ellis gave Jay a smile tinged with apology and squeezed Jay's hand. "I'm fine. I'm right sorry for dragging you out. I didn't want to risk falling into the lake or something stupid. Is Han okay?"

"Eh, don't worry about it." Jay's pitch became strained. "He knows the deal. How did you end up all the way down here, anyway?"

Ellis rose slowly to his feet and slid his hand to Jay's elbow, loosely wrapping his fingers beneath it. "It's my own fault. I wasn't paying attention."

"Tiberius dragged you off?"

Ellis' lips tightened. He didn't want to place all the blame on his dog. He should have paid more attention; Ellis had memorised just about every route he needed for his life and still Tiberius had managed to take him well outside his own territory. "Call it a combined effort, then."

Jay huffed as they started to walk. "You can't be so careless."

"Well it's not *all* me," Ellis groused. "This has got to stop. What if he takes me into someone else's territory and they aren't all that lenient about it? Or if we wind up so far away from home that I can't work out where we are and the sun comes up?"

Jay hissed softly. "Maybe he just needs a bit of re-training? Is that a thing?"

"Maybe. Training's ongoing."

"I'll look into it," Jay assured him. "Leave it with me. I'll catch up with you at the gallery tomorrow and let you know where we stand."

Ellis gave Jay's elbow a light squeeze. "You know I'd be up shit creek without you, don't you?"

Jay laughed. "No, you'd do fine. I know you, Ellis. You built a business in the heart of Mayfair, and you never let your dad, going blind, or dying stop you. You don't let shit get in your way, sweetie. You've got balls the size of most men's heads. We'll figure this out, and everything will be fine."

Ellis was too cold to argue.

TWO

JAY WALKED Ellis to the vampire's front door, made sure he got inside, and jogged through to Park Lane to find a taxi. By the time he got home it was almost three in the morning, and the fare stung his wallet for being out and about while the Tube was shut down.

His own apartment - well, technically Han's - was the other side of London, and on the wrong side of the river. It suited Han fine, since he worked in the City, but for Jay it made for a dependence on public transport which usually ate over half an hour out of his day. He was aware that was something of a meagre complaint that paled in comparison to living with breathtaking views over the Thames, but sometimes it was the little things in life that irked the most.

He nodded to the 24-hour concierge as he hurried through the vast, hotel-like lobby, and was grateful that the building didn't have lift operators like some 1930's department store. By the time Jay emerged onto Han's floor he'd just about managed to tug his hair into some semblance of shape. The sweat helped.

Jay eased his key into the door and went inside as quietly as he could. He shed his coat and shoes by the door, and fumbled his way through the flat to the bedroom. Not for the first time, he offered silent thanks that his sight wasn't like this all the time. God alone knew how Ellis coped with it.

By the time Jay made it to the bedroom his eyes had begun to make out shapes and lines from the light given off by LEDs dotted around the place: phones charging; television on standby; clock on the bedside table. Such small lights, yet they were plenty to see by.

Jay closed the bedroom door and peeled his clothes off.

"You're late," Han said.

Jay froze, absurdly guilty for a split second. "Not late. I just had to nip out." He dropped his shirt and peeled his socks off.

"Ellis?"

"Yeah." Jay sighed. "Sorry, baby. He got lost. Tiberius was acting up again."

He heard Han's slight, exasperated huff before Han said, "It's okay."

Jay shrugged his trousers off and abandoned them on the floor. He crossed the bedroom to his own side of the bed, clambered in under the duvet, and snuggled up to Han's warm, naked body. He saw the outline of Han's cheek and the spike of his hair in the dark, and rested his cheek against Han's arm. "You're upset," he breathed.

Han pursed his lips. "Maybe. But not at you. Not at him." He lifted his hand and brushed his fingers through Jay's hair. "The situation. I never made you work this late, and my new PA is far less sexy than you. She makes lousy tea, too."

Jay laughed quietly. "It's just Tiberius. We'll work it out, then I'll be back before midnight and *stay* home."

"I'll believe it when I see it," Han said dryly. He didn't sound bitter, but Jay didn't want to find out where the tipping point would be.

"I promise."

JAY HURRIED through the shopping centre at the top of Bond Street station and zipped around the corner down the narrow and mostly pedestrian-free Gilbert Street. It was lunch time already, so he wound his way through narrow streets lined with red brick buildings to avoid the deli and restaurant queues which made Davies Street a navigation hazard. It added a few minutes to his jog, but reduced the stress from being late.

The O'Neill Gallery was buried halfway along Brook's Mews amid bare trees and subtle entrances to far larger, far wealthier stores. Bricks were still red, but less vibrant, and glass was in short supply. Although Ellis had leased the space and built his business a few years before he'd become a vampire, the location seemed ideal for someone who didn't want to be observed overly much on his route to and from work.

Jay dug out his keys as he reached the black lacquered wooden doors and unlocked them.

Only forty minutes late, all told. Not bad! Although customers never really showed up until three or four in the afternoon, Jay hadn't made it to Personal Assistant to the CEO of Jade Enterprises by being a slacker, and he wasn't about to turn into one now that he'd jumped ship to an employer who wasn't his husband.

Jay propped the doors open then hurried to the security panel to enter the disarm code. The panel beeped with cheer as though it hadn't been ready to notify the Met of a break-in, and Jay puffed out his cheeks. He had a whole sixty seconds to sort out the alarm after opening the doors, but it always seemed like an achievement.

The gallery looked like it was the right way up, which was a good start to the day, unlike waking up to find that said CEO of Jade Enterprises had slipped off to work in the morning without a kiss goodbye.

Jay chewed his lip while he flicked the lights on. Maybe Han had overslept himself and been forced to rush to the office. It wasn't unusual for Jay to go back to sleep after Han left for the day, but for Han not to even wake him?

Maybe he'd tried and Jay had slept through it.

Jay moved to the window to open the louvre blinds, although it didn't let in much more light than the door in this poky little Mews.

The gallery was just as intact now the lights were on as it had been in darkness, but Jay walked around it just to be sure. Ellis favoured open areas and preferred to sell paintings rather than sculpture, so for the most part the interior was one large room with the works dotted along the walls to give each its own personal space. Currently they had an eclectic selection which ranged from a young artist who used the painstaking method of glazing oils in thin layers to create breathtaking depth, to a modern legend whose technique utilised ink, paper, and high velocity.

The centre of the gallery was occupied by broad steps that led up to the mezzanine level, and an elevator shaft which provided access for those unable to use the stairs. It had cost much of Ellis' budget to install the lift, but he had insisted. While it was been something Ellis wanted to do to aid mobility throughout the gallery, it had proved a shrewd business move too: plenty of customers sought the O'Neill Gallery because they could get around it where older, pokier, or more traditional galleries never bothered.

Satisfied that the shop was open and hadn't been burgled, Jay hopped up the stairs and through another black lacquered door into the office, which was as neat and tidy as the public areas.

Ellis' desk faced the door. It was a plain thing with sturdy white legs and a white painted wooden top. It housed his vast braille keyboard and display, but he had a screen hooked up to his computer so that Jay or customers could also see what he referred to if necessary. Jay's own desk was to the left of the door where anyone entering had to pass it, and he kept it as tidy as Ellis' own but with the added touch of a photo of Han tucked up against his monitor.

Jay woke his computer, made a cup of tea, and dropped into his chair to get started.

He had a gift for research. Jay was a master of accumulating information and comparing it for analysis. When he had worked for Han his talent had been put to use finding the best travel costs, hotel prices, and dirt on their competitors. Ellis didn't travel, rented his own apartment, and competition in the art world was a far less predictable creature. The opportunity to stretch his muscles before they atrophied completely wasn't to be missed, and Jay threw himself into finding the best dog trainer in the city that Ellis' budget would allow.

He read pages of reviews and jotted down notes in a spreadsheet he made purely for his hastily-constructed comparison chart. By the time he was ready to select the top three trainers, his tea was finished and the cup cold.

Jay called all three and left voicemail for two. The third outright refused to work evenings, so she was an easy one to cross from his list.

The service entrance intercom buzzed, and Jay turned away from his phone to check it. A middle-aged man in coveralls was referring to a handheld computer.

Jay sighed and pressed his intercom button. "O'Neill Gallery."

The man looked up and said, "Delivery."

"No problem. Come in." Jay held the unlock button down until the driver pulled the door open, then hurried down the stairs to go meet him.

Jay chatted amiably with the driver and kept the door open for him as he fetched four cardboard-wrapped canvases in from his van. Jay gave his signature on the handheld's huge screen, then ferried the paintings to the elevator, and from there up to the office. He was checking the identifying stickers against his printed manifest when his desk phone rang, and Jay set the paper down to go grab the call.

"O'Neill Gallery, Jay Newfield speaking. How can I help you?"

The voice which answered was deep and soft, with an easy East End accent to it. "Hi. I'm returning a voicemail?" He made it sound like a question, as though he wasn't certain that was what he was doing. "I'm Randall. Carter," he added. "You were looking for a dog trainer?"

"Oh, of course." Jay smiled as though Carter were in the room. It was the best way to inject warmth into his voice, and it went a long way to get him what he wanted in phone calls. "Thanks for returning my call so quickly. I'm calling on behalf of my employer, Ellis O'Neill. He's unavailable right now, but his guide dog is behaving a little erratically lately and I was hoping you might be available to look into it for us."

"Sure. Yeah, no problem." Carter sounded eager to please, which was always nice in a man. "When's good for you? Uh, him?"

Jay bit his lip. Here came the crunch. "Well, as I'm sure you can imagine, as my employer runs a thriving art gallery-" Jay wished just for a moment that there was at least *one* customer beyond the office door to back up this claim "-he's a very busy man during the day. Would you be at all able to work evenings?"

"Yeah," Carter said without a moment's hesitation. "Evenings are fine. Whereabouts are you?"

"Mayfair. Brook's Mews. Right by Claridge's. You can't miss us."

Carter made *mmmhmm* sounds. The sort of noises people made

when they were scrabbling about for a pen. Then he said "What time?"

"Shall we say 8PM? You can do this evening, yes?"

"Yeah, yeah. Eight this evening. Ellis O'Neill. Got it. I'll be there."

"Wonderful. Thank you, Mr. Carter."

Jay hung up and texted Ellis, then got back to unpacking the delivery.

THREE

RANDALL PREFERRED to work during the day of course, but evenings and weekends were far more usual. It was when most of his clients weren't at work themselves, and as a freelancer he was beholden to the availability of the paying customer.

This would be the first time he had been called to train a dog at an art gallery, though. An art gallery with a blind owner, too, if the dog was trained as a service animal.

It was highly unusual for a guide dog to act out. They were paired with a handler in a process that took several weeks, and if the pairing didn't work out the dog got moved on to try out a new potential handler. Randall hoped the customer's dog wasn't ill; that kind of news would be devastating for the owner.

Not for the first time, Randall was grateful that his senses were only slightly better than a human's while wearing their shape. London could have its own *interesting* odours, and if he had to encounter them with his wolf's nose he could well regret it. Brook's Mews looked tiny on the map, and he prayed it wasn't a small alleyway lined with litter.

He approached from Davies Street, and was pleased to find that Brook's Mews was a reasonably wide service road lined with trees which were bare this time of year. The winter was unseasonably warm, but nature was hard to fool; these slender boughs had shed their leaves long ago. Randall walked along the Mews until he found the subtle Claridge's staff entrance Jay had told him about, then found the black lacquered door snuggled nearby, set a little back from the pavement and with a silvery sign next to the door which read "The O'Neill Gallery" in a simple, clean typeface.

Randall paused at the door and placed his hand on it. While he'd never been to an art gallery before, he somehow had in his head an image of vast glass buildings with modern architecture and daring signage. This place was discreet, in a building which was likely over a hundred years old, and didn't seem the sort of place to invite strangers in off the street. How were customers to even find it, buried away down here?

He pushed, and the door swept open. It was heavy, but moved well on its hinges, and the air within was warm. Randall hopped inside and closed the door to keep as much heat from escaping as possible.

He caught his breath as he looked into the gallery. The space was larger than he thought it would be from the outside, and every wall was dotted with paintings. He could see vibrant colours and subtle shades, and no one picture claimed dominance over the room. A beautiful portrait of an elderly woman sat alongside inked outlines of horses, which in turn led on to a vast single red poppy. Randall stepped further into the gallery and picked out the faint scent of a dog somewhere among the fragrances of long-gone visitors and the lingering vanilla from some sort of diffuser somewhere.

Movement at the top of some stairs drew his eye, and a lithe man with upward-facing brown hair hopped down the steps toward him. "Good evening. Welcome to The O'Neill Gallery. How may I help you?"

His voice matched the phone call from earlier in the day. "Jay?" Randall said as he offered his hand to the taller man. "I'm Randall Carter. I hope I'm not too early?"

"Oh, hey!" Jay broke into a relaxed smile. "No, it's fine. Thank you for coming. Can I take your coat?"

"Oh, no. It's fine. Thank you." Randall always felt that letting people take his coat, or fetch him cups of tea, or do any of the other things they always offered to do was somehow an imposition. At least if he kept his coat Jay wouldn't have to run around after him or fetch it for him later on.

"No worries. Would you follow me?" Jay beckoned, then hopped right back up the steps, taking them two at a time with ease.

Randall grabbed the hand rail and followed, hurrying to catch up with the lanky assistant. Up here the only non-dog scent he could detect was Jay's cologne, which Jay thankfully used as an accent rather than a bath.

Jay led him to another lacquer door which already hung open, and stepped inside. "Mr. Carter is here," he said to the figure behind one of two desks, and he gestured for Randall to go past him.

Randall stepped around Jay to face his client, and his breath rushed from him.

O'Neill was gorgeous. He looked to be around thirty years old, with soft hair that fell in tousled waves and covered his collar. His skin was pale, white, with pinkish lips and barely-tamed stubble framing his insouciant features. His eyes were hidden behind dark glasses with rectangular frames.

O'Neill's lips twitched. He said nothing.

Jay cleared his throat. "I'll get tea." He sneaked out of the room past Randall, and Randall heard him laugh to himself as he hurried down the stairs.

Randall tried to take his eyes off O'Neill long enough to refuse the tea, but Jay was gone.

"Mr. Carter," O'Neill said. "Thank you for coming so late." He stood and offered his hand across the desk.

Randall was spurred into action. He closed the distance to give O'Neill his hand as he shook his head. "You're welcome. It's no problem. How can I help?"

This close to the desk, O'Neill's dog was unmissable. An adult male German Shepherd, he lay patiently to the left of O'Neill's chair, chin on his front paws. His eyes swivelled up to take in Randall's presence, but he didn't cower or back away as most dogs might in the presence of a wolf shifter; instead his ears lowered in brief deference and he closed his eyes again.

O'Neill withdrew his hand and sat, gesturing to the chair facing his desk as he did so. "Please, call me Ellis. I don't stand for all that formal stuff. This isn't the nineteenth century." Ellis spoke with some subtle flecks of a Yorkshire accent, and his smile came easily to him.

Randall wondered what his lips tasted like.

He sat in the chair he'd been offered. "Randall," he supplied. His voice sounded hoarse, so he cleared his throat. "Sorry. So, um. Is this the dog?"

Ellis laughed. "Aye. Tiberius. He's four now, and I've had him a couple of years. Don't get me wrong, he's always had a few quirks, but he's a good dog. He works hard."

Randall rubbed his jaw, surreptitiously bringing his shaken hand close to his nose. He couldn't detect any scent from Ellis, nor from where the man had touched him. Surely this close, in the man's own office, he should have picked something up by now?

It was as though Ellis weren't even here.

"Um." Randall blinked. "Right. Well, for today, then, what I want to do is go over your situation, Tiberius' behaviour, and what you'd like to happen. After that can we go out for a walk together?"

Ellis' lips twitched again.

Randall's skin flushed. His cheeks felt like they were on fire. "Uh, with Tiberius. So I can observe him working," he added, the words tumbling from him like they were ashamed to be in the same room.

"Absolutely." Ellis grinned.

Randall almost welcomed the distraction of Jay's return, tilting toward him when he heard his footsteps. He carried an eggbox-style tray of tea in takeaway cups, and each burgundy cup was capped with a plastic lid. As Randall turned further, he caught sight of the kettle and fridge in the corner of the office.

Had Jay gone all the way to Davies Street so that Randall and Ellis could be alone?

"Thanks, Jay," Ellis said.

"You're welcome." Jay set the tray down and had to twist the cups to prise them out of the tray. He placed one by Ellis' hand and nudged Ellis' index finger with it, then offered another to Randall. "I didn't add any milk or sugar to yours. I forgot to ask what you'd like. But we have both here." Jay gave him an impish grin which cemented Randall's suspicion, then pulled his own cup from the tray and popped the tray itself into one of several bright-coloured recycling bins. "I need to go and do a thing that is downstairs."

Ellis' fingers closed around the cup. "Aye. You go do that thing, Jay. Thanks."

"You're welcome." Jay scurried out again.

Randall bit his lip and tried to figure out which of his questions he wanted to ask first.

"I heard his footsteps," Ellis said. He found the lid with his other hand and plucked it off. A puff of vapour escaped.

"What?" Randall blinked. "How-"

"You were wondering how I knew it was Jay?" Ellis chuckled. "We have a kettle here. He didn't need to leave to get tea, so he obviously thinks I fancy you and is trying to give us some privacy." Now the tips of Randall's ears were burning too. "The nearest place to get a cup of tea in reasonable speed is Costa, and assuming they aren't heaving it shouldn't take him more than ten minutes to get there and back. People who don't work here don't come in through the door, head straight for the stairs, and then trot up them and immediately approach the office. That and today he's wearing his trainers, so the footfalls are soft. That means he was probably late for work this morning, because he prefers to take more time over his wardrobe than dragging on a pair of trainers." Ellis sipped his tea. "It would also make sense for him to be late this morning, as I had to call him out in the wee small hours last night due to Tiberius leading me astray."

Randall squirmed in his seat. He thought he was usually observant, but Ellis seemed to have him beat. And he was so casual about Jay leaving them to their "privacy". Did this happen a lot?

"Relax. Jay doesn't try to set me up with every customer, artist, agent, or supplier who walks in here." Ellis' lips twitched. "You obviously get his seal of approval. Regardless, we're bordering on inappropriate behaviour here, so if you don't mind I shall leave any and all flirting until we are outside a customer-provider relationship."

Randall felt like he hadn't had a second to catch his breath. He was the centre of a whirlwind, and it was zipping along without any input from him. "Right," he said, his voice faint.

"What do you know about retinitis pigmentosa?"

"Uh." Randall tried to nudge his mind back on track. "I've never heard of it. Sorry." Was it paint? A dog-handling technique? Some kind of sex position?

"Milk is in the fridge. The sugar's by the kettle." Ellis sipped again as Randall spurred himself out of his chair and went to get both. "Not all RP is the same. It's genetic. You generally reach adulthood before you start going blind, but not always. Anyway." He took another mouthful and swallowed before continuing. "I was a bit clumsy through Uni. Didn't really think anything of it. I never learned to drive, and I didn't really notice the peripheral vision was going until after I'd started the business. Anyway, point is it only gets worse, can't be cured, and my peripheral and night vision were the first things to go. My light vision's piss-poor too, but at least there *is* some."

Randall added a splash of milk and a spoon of sugar to his tea while he listened, then returned everything to where it came from, including himself. He sat and cradled the cup. "So…" He hesitated. Would it be insensitive to ask questions, or was Ellis giving him permission by raising the subject first?

"I looked into getting a guide dog pretty quickly. They're basically the Ferrari of mobility options once you're visually impaired. A cane's all well and good, but a dog will get you there faster, and I didn't want to be dependent on Jay, lose a couple of hours out of my day, or rely on taxis all the time. I got paired up with Tiberius and we were going great guns at first. After all, they let me keep him." Ellis flashed a wry smile.

"Oh." Randall felt like he'd just had a minor epiphany. Ellis told him about his blindness because Randall had said he wanted to go over Ellis' situation. The customer was more on the ball than he was, and Randall felt like a bloody idiot. What the hell had he been thinking? "Right. Um. And since then?"

"Good as gold, to start with. But for the past few weeks he's been growling at strangers, taking me off-route, refusing to do as he's told. I mean, at first I assumed it was his Intelligent Disobedience kicking in, but it just got more and more out of hand. Last night I ended up in the middle of St. James' Park, but what if he takes me further? I don't really go outside Mayfair any more, and I can't keep calling Jay out at 3AM. It's not fair on him." Ellis' rakish smile had seemed a perpetual fixture, but it faded as he talked, and he seemed smaller for it somehow.

"Dogs prefer routine," Randall said. "Is he on a regular schedule?"

Ellis tipped his head. It made his glossy hair tumble forward, and he brushed it back with one hand when he lifted it again. "Aye. We're up same time every day, and we're usually to bed the same time too, if we don't go wandering after hours." His tone suggested that the wandering he referred to wasn't at Ellis' command.

"I don't want to do myself out of a job, but is there a reason you haven't called in the Guide Dog Mobility Instructor?"

Ellis paused. Randall watched as his body tensed and his expression became flat and guarded. He looked like a cornered deer, just for a moment.

What was so damning about that question?

"They aren't all that keen on evenings," Ellis said, his voice carefully neutral.

"Okay." Randall nibbled the rim of his cardboard cup, then gulped down his tea. He couldn't press the customer on that. Maybe it'd come out in a couple of weeks' time, but for now he didn't want to lose a client over something that was probably minor. Maybe Ellis had fallen out with the Instructor or something. "Well, I'm happy to take you on, but I can't give a timeline until we see how Tiberius works out and about. I can't guarantee success. It could be that they paired you poorly after all, and he might end up going back to the training centre for re-homing."

Ellis leaned back in his seat, mouth curving downward in dismay. "I'm not re-homing my dog, Randall. I love him to pieces!"

Randall lifted his hand in defence, only to remember that Ellis couldn't see it. Or maybe he could. Hadn't he said he was only night blind? Was the light in his office enough for him to see by, even with sunglasses on? "I'm going to do everything I can to fix this, I promise."

"Good. Shall we go on that walk?"

Randall bobbed his head quickly. "Yeah. Let's do that."

Best to do it before he could wedge his foot any further into his own mouth.

FOUR

THEY EMERGED out into the Mews, and suddenly Randall had a moment's insight into Ellis' situation. From the well-lit interior to a road with only one street lamp up the far end, Randall was blinded for a few seconds, while Ellis had simply continued on his way.

Ellis stopped and tilted his head. "Randall?"

"Sorry. Uh." He rubbed his eyes and blinked, then hurried to Ellis' side. "There's no light down this road."

"It's very discreet," Ellis agreed with a crooked grin. "Sorry. I've usually only got Tiberius with me when I come outside. You areet now?"

"Yeah, yeah. I'm fine."

They got started again, and Tiberius plodded dutifully along, his ears swivelling around as he listened both for obstacles ahead and his pack leader at his side. Tiberius was paying plenty of attention to Ellis, and walking alongside him at a matched pace.

"Where shall we go?" Ellis asked.

They passed other galleries as they walked toward the ornate Victorian street lamp. Ellis' location wasn't so poor after all, if this tiny little street was jammed with other galleries. Maybe this was Mayfair's little secret?

"Any route you'd normally use is fine." Randall slid his hands into his coat pockets.

"Great." Ellis' hair flopped as he nodded. "Let's head down to

Berkeley Square Gardens. It's on my way home." After they turned right at the end of the Mews, Ellis added "Have you experience of working with the visually impaired, then?"

"No. Not really. Why'd you ask?"

"Not everyone knows that guide dogs come with a Mobility Instructor."

Randall bit his lip. "Oh, well. I did some research before I came."

"Before I'd committed as a customer?" Ellis' chin lifted. "You're diligent. You're also not treating me like I'm a cripple, which is refreshing. More research?"

"Well you're not missing limbs, are you?" Randall laughed faintly. If Ellis had been a shifter it might be another story altogether. He hadn't ever met a disabled shifter, but then he'd only known a handful. Still, this was London in the 21st century, and even hearing Ellis use the word *cripple* was weird.

Probably about as weird as hearing *faggot* or *darkie*.

Randall's humour dispersed as his comprehension kicked in. Ellis was used to being discriminated against, and Randall had brushed it aside as readily as others might look the other way if Randall spoke out about racism or homophobia.

"Oh, god," he breathed. "I'm sorry. I just meant-" He broke off. What *had* he meant? That he'd think of a paraplegic as *crippled*? That was ridiculous. Wasn't it?

The wolf inside him grumbled at the thought of a predator who couldn't hunt, and he squirmed uncomfortably.

"It's my fault," Ellis said. "I put words in your mouth. The sighted tend to assume that being unable to see also robs you of intelligence or competence. But by asking you that question I made an assumption, and I'm sorry."

Randall swallowed. "What assumption?"

"That you shared those attitudes just because you can see." Ellis' grin returned with ease.

Randall snorted at that. "I think we're just digging a hole here."

"Yeah." Ellis sighed, turning wistful. "Still, it *is* nice to be treated like a human being, Randall. Thank you."

"Any time." Randall fidgeted within his pockets. "Though... Is it okay if I ask something?"

"I dunno. Why don't you ask it and find out?"

"How do you cope? I mean-" He sucked in air. "You went to University, you own an art gallery... You sell art, right? So how do you choose what to sell? Can you see well enough in there to pick things out? You don't seem to sell much in the way of sculpture, so-" He broke off again to prevent himself from babbling, and looked worriedly over at Ellis, afraid he'd offended the taller man.

Ellis shrugged. "I have a degree in Fine Art. I always loved art, but I bloody stunk as an artist, so I went for the next best thing. Dad's fairly minted, so I scrounged a few bob off him and came down South to start a gallery. Nowadays I handle the business end of things and Jay does all the selection. I don't really like to take my glasses off indoors and let the light in; it's not very clear, and I get more frustrated than anything else. It's kind of like some tosspot smeared Vaseline all over the lens and there's a tiny spot that's still there. It's like trying to read a book through a pinhole. Pain in the arse. I'd rather just not be bothered with it."

Randall looked to Tiberius as they crossed a small street. The conversation was interrupted by a short series of instructions from Ellis as man and dog worked in harmony to guide them beneath the narrow brick walls of Bourdon Street which, despite having a name was little more than an alleyway with a narrow pavement along one edge that Ellis didn't bother attempting to use. There was no sign that Tiberius wasn't doing his job, or that he was about to tear off on a rampage of growling at people - not that there were many on the streets. The most Randall had seen on their walk so far had been inside the bars and pubs they had passed, to which Tiberius paid no mind.

"Anyway, carry on," Ellis said to him once they'd navigated past the winding junction.

"He seems to be doing the business," Randall admitted. "Not that I want to do myself out of work."

Ellis nodded. "Oh, he does. He's amazing. It's just when it goes wrong it goes properly wrong, you know?"

"I can imagine, yeah."

They continued all the way to the wrought iron railings of Berkeley Square Gardens, where Ellis and Tiberius came to a halt. Ellis rested his right hand on the locked gate, which only came up to his hip. It was as ornately wrought as the rest of the iron in Mayfair. A discreet sign on the railing to the gate's right gave a telephone number for the park's manager.

Randall was pretty sure Stepney Green didn't have a "park manager", and if you put his phone number by the gate he'd be getting drunken calls at all hours.

Ellis had mentioned the money came from his dad, and he didn't sound like your typical posh West Ender. He'd picked up a lot of the area's accent, but the Yorkshire was still there, brewing under the surface. Still, Randall found himself wondering whether the art business paid well, or whether at the end of the night Ellis went home to a bedsit in Clapham. Did the art dealer feel as out of place in this manicured spot surrounded by fine Georgian apartments, or had he settled in like a duck returned to its favourite pond?

"This is it," Ellis said simply. "It closes earlier in the autumn, alas, but in the summer it's open until nine."

"It's nice." Randall looked into the park, a flat space with trees and sculptures, and some sort of bandstand or building in the centre.

Ellis laughed easily. "It's a good place to sit and read, if you like to do so in public to show off how well-read you are. Come along." He brushed his fingers up Randall's arm, and wrapped them around his elbow.

The touch fired all kinds of haywire signals through Randall's body. His breath quickened, and his groin stirred. He bit his lip hard to try and focus, and said nothing while Ellis turned the whole party around and across the street, back the way they had come.

"Are you all right there?"

"Yeah." Randall's fists clenched in his pockets until the nails dug against his palms.

"Well, obviously he's going to behave himself. It's probably because you're here." Ellis didn't seem too bothered by this. "Still, you reckon it's something you can handle, not having witnessed the issue first-hand?"

"I'm willing to try." Randall could have kicked himself for sounding so spineless. "I don't want to build up any expectations-"

"I understand. Until you actually observe the problem you can't know what might be causing it." Ellis' fingers squeezed Randall's elbow. "Where do we go from here?"

My place? Yours? Randall had to fight to keep his brain within the context of their conversation. "Uh, well. It might benefit me to see him earlier in the day, when he's more alert."

"I'm sorry, Dave. I'm afraid I can't do that." Ellis' head shook slightly. "The gallery is jam-packed early evenings most days, and sometimes well into the wee hours if we have a launch or other event planned. This is really the best time for me, if that's all right?"

"Yeah, sure thing." He bit his tongue, then added "Dave?"

"Don't tell me you've never watched 2001: A Space Odyssey?"

"I haven't seen it."

Ellis' eyebrows climbed above the frames of his glasses. "It's a work of art. Which, you know, not everyone wants from a film. Cinema audiences like to be told a story, but 2001 provides music and visuals and asks you to construct your own, if you feel that way inclined. There's little dialogue in it, so what there was has become reasonably famous." His head tipped toward Randall. "You've never even heard that line?"

Randall couldn't help feeling like he was committing some grave sin. "Well, er. I don't watch much TV, or go to the pictures often."

"Oh?" Ellis' head faced forward again. "Mind if I ask why?"

Randall shrugged. "I dunno. Cinemas are loud and expensive, and most TV's just rubbish, innit? Soaps or reality shows. None of it engages. It's like it's just there to-" Randall drew a breath, then let it out slowly. "I dunno. Like it's there to help people waste their lives."

Ellis' eyebrows rose again. "Very perceptive of you," he murmured. He sounded impressed. "Marx suggested that religion was the opium of the people, but I think were he alive today he would describe entertainment that way instead. The sigh of the oppressed creature, the heart of a heartless world. The spirit of a spiritless situation. With millions living in misery, modern entertainment provides a nicotine patch to soothe the unhappiness and tell the people that life is acceptable."

Randall blinked at him. "Christ, that's bleak."

"That's Marx for you." Ellis chortled and gave Randall's elbow another light squeeze. "Although as one business owner to another, would you say that vegging out in front of the television would contribute to your productivity?" He didn't wait for Randall to answer. "No, of course you wouldn't. I have customers through my doors, if you will pardon that mental image, who own football clubs, multinational corporations, perhaps even small countries, and not a single one of them lists television or cinema as a hobby. They don't have the time. Too busy. But some films, some television, is art. 2001 is most definitely art. You should watch it, perhaps. If you feel like it. Though I'm not sure it would be the same experience on Blu-ray."

Randall dipped his head. "I'll see what I can do."

Ellis smirked softly. "That's a very polite answer. Your mum'd be proud." He slowed to a halt at the gallery's doors and released Randall's elbow. "When would you like to begin with Tiberius?"

"Uh." Randall looked up at the doors. They were closed now, but light still trickled out around the edges of the window's blinds. "Monday?"

"Monday it is, then." Ellis offered his hand, and Randall took it.

Where Randall's hand was hot from having been balled in his coat pocket for the entire walk, Ellis' was cold with exposure to the night air. "You should go in," Randall said quickly. "You've gotten really cold."

"The perils of wandering around without gloves on at this time of year," Ellis mourned. "See you on Monday, then."

"Will do."

Ellis unlocked the door and disappeared into the gallery, and Randall rubbed his face once the door was closed.

There was no denying it. Randall fancied the pants off his client.

FIVE

ELLIS LOCKED the door and drew a breath. He could hear Randall's still-hurried heart as the trainer outside slowly withdrew from the door. Tiberius' own heartbeat remained strong and calm at his side, and his breathing sent gentle tremors along the harness.

It took another second to locate Jay's heart, and he smiled a little, glad that he'd waited.

"Jay," he called. "Are you in?"

"You know I am, dear." Jay's answer was spoken, not shouted, yet Ellis heard it clearly.

He chuckled and spurred Tiberius toward the stairs, hand finding the rail before he allowed the dog to continue.

"Spill the beans," Jay said once Ellis sat at his desk. "How did it go?"

Ellis' hands drifted across to the braille display, and he tapped at it to wake his computer. "About as well as expected, I suppose. Tiberius was an absolute model of obedience and training, so the poor man's got absolutely nothing to work with."

"Ugh." Jay sounded oddly disappointed.

"It's not your fault. You found a trainer, and he seems like he might be a good one." Ellis tried to give a reassuring smile. "Besides, that isn't the end of it. He's popping over on Monday to begin some training exercises regardless, just to be sure."

"Good!"

Ellis' fingers paused on the keys. "Okay, what's going on?"

"Nothing! I mean, he's adorable, and totally has the hots for you, but other than that?" Jay cracked his knuckles. "Absolutely nothing."

Ellis' thoughts turned to the myriad of spikes in Randall's heartbeats throughout the evening, and the little gasps and telling pauses he'd given, microscopic at best to human ears but like beacons in the night to Ellis' hearing. "I do suspect he finds me passingly appealing," he admitted. "But I'm not going to take him out on a date, Jay."

"Oh you are such a sourpuss!" Jay's chair creaked. "You like him, right?"

Ellis' brow raised. "What makes you think that?"

"Because Tiberius didn't act out, but you've booked Randall to come back anyway."

"I have trained you well, young Padawan," Ellis grumbled. "He has a beautiful voice. And nice warm hands."

"Right. You talked to him about non-dog stuff, yeah?"

"Aye."

"And on a scale of Gandhi to Wilde, how pretentious were you?"

Ellis scowled a little and scrolled through his inbox before he answered. "Somewhere around Joyce," he admitted.

Jay groaned. "He's your dog trainer, not a customer!"

"I don't care if the dog trainer thinks I'm a wazzock. It isn't like we're going to be all flowers and serenades. I'll see him for a week or two, then that'll be it."

"It doesn't have to be!" Jay sighed. "He's a cutie. You're a cutie. You could be cuties together."

"And then?" Ellis shook his head and skim-read a few emails. "We had a delivery today?"

"Yes. Don't change the subject." He heard Jay move out of his chair and over to the storage unit they both called 'goods in'. "Four pieces, all from Nolan. You can't go through life alone just because you don't need to breathe anymore."

"Oh, you don't think the blood drinking and sunlight allergy is an issue? Be still my already-still heart. Jay is going to find me the man of my dreams." Ellis rolled his eyes, even though Jay couldn't see the gesture. "Four pieces? He's eager. Is he running out of storage in his flat?" He listened as Jay cut through cardboard and plastic to unwrap the delivery.

"No idea. Maybe he's just excited that you've agreed to represent him and would like to put you off before you even display anything." Jay stopped talking as the noise of unwrapping subsided, and instead made a soft sound of surprise. "Or he'd like to blow our socks off," he added more gently.

Ellis pulled a drawer open and slid the braille display into it to clear his desk. It was a snug fit, and he had to wedge the display between diagonal corners to get it in there, but once it was safe and secure he closed the drawer and felt around the rest of his desk to be sure there was nothing on it that shouldn't be. "All right," he said when he was done. "From the top."

Jay came closer and settled a painting on the mostly-cleared desk. Ellis didn't make out the heavy thud of a frame; instead it was more the softened thump of stretched canvas. "Woman on Horse," Jay recited. "Oil on Canvas. Unframed. Varnished."

Varnished meant that the oils had dried completely - or that the artist had gone ahead and applied varnish before they were, in which case it would crack. Ellis doubted that Nolan would varnish prematurely; Nolan was an experienced painter.

While the odds were slender that putting his fingers all over a delivered piece would smudge it, Ellis far preferred to handle works which were already colour-fast. He ran his fingers along the edge of the canvas, and then drew them in toward the centre, searching for Nolan's focal point while his fingers detected every single stroke of the brush.

Ellis kept a few secrets from the world at large. His existence as a vampire was something only Jay knew of, and if the Council ever found out about that there'd be hell to pay. He had other secrets, kept even from Jay, but the tool in his arsenal which allowed him to maintain some semblance of productivity was his power.

There wasn't really any better word for it than that. After Jonas had turned him almost a year ago, he'd explained about the vampire's power while they tried to work out what exactly Ellis' was. Apparently something about the way vampire blood interacted with a human's body or mind - or perhaps both - blossomed into a single, unique flower which was forever more at that individual's disposal.

For Jonas that had been an impossible way with words: he could understand and communicate in any language he encountered without any prior exposure whatsoever. Jonas had written it off as worthless, but then Jonas had written off most things in life as worthless. He spun tales of vampires across London with other, far more "useful" powers: superior speed; mind control; shape-changing. He said he'd met a vampire in Limehouse who could walk through walls, and another who turned into a wolf.

Jonas' problem was that he'd been full of shit. After he had turned Ellis he rapidly lost interest in taking care of his fledgling's needs. And now he was gone.

Ellis' power wasn't like Jonas'. It gave, but it mocked, too. When he touched an object, Ellis was able to witness key moments in its history as though he had been present. He would feel what those there had felt, and he would see events unfold with sight unavailable to him through his own eyes.

It was Ellis' last and only means of discerning colour or detail.

His fingers stirred the lingering impressions from Nolan's passion, and finally light flooded Ellis' mind.

Nolan worked hard. He fussed over details, ever the perfectionist. This painting was a fragment of love, although frustration certainly bled through during its creation. The underpainting was awash with yellows, golds, browns; a monochromatic outline as Nolan - pudgy, pretty Nolan - worked out his values before he went any further. He used watercolours for his underpainting, Ellis saw, and once Nolan was satisfied he turned to his oils.

Woman on Horse. There was no woman; no horse. That was part of Nolan's joke. He painted gruesome vistas with troubled skies and elements of surrealism, and yet his emotions while he worked were almost always ones Ellis would categorise as positive. Love. Happiness. Contentment. Ellis' theory was that Nolan purged himself via his work, and it seemed to have that effect; Nolan was one of the more laid-back and pleasant artists on Ellis' books.

Time fled by as layer after layer grew on the canvas. Nolan's work was enough to make a grown man weep if he dared stop to think about it for too long. London's South Bank unfurled across the underpainting in a gross reflection of itself, the Eye looming over all, the water of the Thames black and threatening. Under Nolan's brush the Royal Festival Hall became a ravenous monster and the National Theatre a machine processing meat. Its walls bled, and its ground product poured into the Thames, which sucked on the endless stream with eager mouths.

The varnish dried.

Ellis' vision drifted to black, and his prison reasserted itself.

"Bloody heck," he whispered.

"Mm. It's a good one, isn't it?" Jay squeezed his shoulder. "Are you okay?"

"Aye. Just-" Ellis lifted his hands away from the surface. "God, if we can't sell this, there's no hope left for humanity. Tell me the rest are as good."

"Let me look." Jay's hand went away, and he walked back over to the goods in stash. There was the soft swish of fingers over canvas, and tiny creaks as Jay sifted through the three remaining paintings. "Wow." He cleared his throat. "Yeah. Yeah, I'd say they are."

"All right. Let's have the next, then." Ellis sat back while Jay switched canvases.

"You're still not shaking me off," Jay laughed. "I'm like a dog with a bone, me. Come on. What's to stop you taking Randall out? You like him, he likes you. Just one date. Live a little."

"And what happens when he sits up in bed one morning and throws the curtains open?"

"Eh." Jay sat again. "Obviously you don't go straight from date to bed, dear. I know you've been off the scene a while, but have some restraint. You just take it easy, and if it looks like it's going somewhere tell him. Who knows? Maybe you could find someone who'd be willing to let you, you know." Jay's tone turned dirty. "Suck on more than just his swizzle-stick."

Ellis snorted. "Pervert."

"You could be partners in every sense," Jay crowed with glee.

"Is this it? Your ultimate goal? Some homoerotic vampire sex fantasy?"

Jay sniggered. "It'd be hot."

"God, where the hell did I find you?" Ellis shook his head, unable to keep the smile from his lips. "Anyway, it's all pointless. It wouldn't work. What happens longer term, when he gets to grow old and I don't?"

"Well, do you know whether you're actually going to live forever and never grow old and all that stuff?"

Ellis tapped his fingers on the arm of his chair, and he leaned back. "Well, no. Jonas said the Council of Elders were all, well, Elders, but-"

"But he was full of shit," Jay stated. "Well maybe you should find out. You can't just carry on not knowing anything. There's got to be enough of them out there to need a Council in the first place."

"And that Council has rules against us letting people find out what we are. You could be in serious danger if they ever work out you know even half the things I've told you." Ellis sighed and brushed hair away from his forehead.

"My lips are sealed, I promise you. I don't want to get eaten. Well, not like *that*."

"And I don't want you to get eaten. Not like *that*." Ellis frowned. "I already feel bad enough that Han hardly gets any time with you."

"Oh don't start that again. It's my choice to work here. You don't hold me hostage. Now get on and fondle the next one." A flip of paper. "Child on Skateboard. Oil on Canvas. Varnished."

Ellis pursed his lips, but said nothing further on the matter. They had work to do, and it was late, so he leaned forward and felt his way around the next canvas.

SIX

RANDALL'S QUESTIONS had to wait until he'd had a full night's sleep.

Well, they didn't *have* to. His pack was always somewhere to be found; Randall simply preferred not to find them unless absolutely necessary.

Their pack wasn't a family unit. They had formed out of necessity, out of a need to survive in a city, and as such their hierarchy was stunted. Added to their wolf instincts was a lifetime of human upbringing, which all culminated in a structure which required an Omega.

Randall was the shortest, the least aggressive, and most empathetic. He was a natural fit for a role which only he understood wouldn't occur in a natural, family-formed pack. Instead they were a rag-tag bunch of lone individuals all trying to prove they were a contender for Alpha, and Briar was some kind of miracle worker for keeping them from spilling violence into the streets. Randall was part of Briar's arsenal. He took the bullying and taunts because it kept the pack sane; kept it thriving.

But he was buggered if he was ever going to *like* it.

It did make deciding who to speak to an easy thing, though. Other pack members may attempt to take out their stresses on him if he approached them, or use his weaker position to leverage whatever they learned from his lack of knowledge to further their own goals.

His choice was simple. He had to go to the top, to someone who already felt secure enough not to worry about whatever inane nonsense Randall took to them.

He approached the garage with his hands stuffed into his pockets. The scent of his pack was strong here, even perceptible to his human nose, and he detected both Preeti and Briar. It was Preeti he was here to see, though, and he strode along the cobbled back-street toward the garage's open doors.

There was a string of cars parked outside already. Older vehicles with rust around the wheel rims or scratches on the paintwork. Preeti's garage was built from the arch of a railway bridge, by simple process of sticking wooden walls at each end of the archway, and the busy line overhead rumbled with slow-moving commuter trains every few minutes. Either side of her garage other arches were blocked up and used for storage or a sandwich shop that wouldn't open until lunchtime.

He walked around a battered old Ford Focus and stepped into the garage. A couple of cars were up on stilts, and he saw Preeti in the bay underneath one of them.

"Preeti," he called.

She pushed safety goggles up into her thick, dark hair and cast him a grin. "Hey, Randall!" She put gloved hands against the floor and vaulted out from the bay, her tiny body swinging through the air like an athlete's. Heavy boots clomped on the concrete and she dragged her gloves off while she walked over to him so that she could offer him a clean hand. "Wotcher!"

Randall gripped her hand, and was drawn into a ferocious bear hug from a woman half his size. He laughed and squeezed around her shoulders. "All right? Busy?"

"I always got time for my little cub, Rand. 'Sup?"

"Shall I put the kettle on?"

"Yeah. Probably won't suit you, though." She laughed and eased the goggles free from her hair, then led him to her office.

Randall followed, unplugged her kettle, and took it to the sink to fill, then set about making the tea while she unstacked a chair for him.

Her office was dingy. Clean, but dated. The plaster had peeled and been painted over too many times to count. There were a couple of missing ceiling tiles, and some of the remainder bore the brownish stains of an air-conditioner leak long gone. Her floor was grey linoleum that had bubbled in one corner. The place was metal and wood, with grey filing cabinets and dark brown desktops, and the only window looked out onto the garage interior. All in all it was a top candidate for sick building syndrome.

The trouble with being a shifter was it didn't exactly lend itself to full-time employment with a white collar company. Most shifters, if they tried to retain some semblance of human living at all, became self-employed, and the cost of living was so high that Preeti saved a fortune sleeping in her own workshop. But Randall wished she'd spend a little of her earnings on tarting the place up a bit. It might draw in customers who could pay more.

He brought the tea over and sat with her, and found her dark almond eyes fixed on his. "Haven't seen you in a couple of days," she said as she took the chipped mug. "Everything okay?"

"Oh, yeah. Clients." He shrugged. "I've got sessions this afternoon, too, so I can't stay forever."

"I don't want forever." She blew on the tea, sending little puffs of vapour into the space between them. "How's your mum?"

"Yeah, she's fine." Randall broke into the same smile he wore every time she asked that question. His mum - maybe his whole family - was alive thanks to Preeti. "Kieran's okay, too. Calming down in his old age, I think," he added.

"Awesome. Tell him to stop being such a prick." She grinned, though. "But you didn't come for a social call, did you?"

"Bloody hell, give me a second to settle in, won't you?" He gave her the side-eye.

"No way, mate. You came 'ere because you want something today. I know you too well."

"Where's Briar?"

Preeti put her mug down. "Hang on."

Before Randall could protest, she jumped to her feet and went out into the garage. "Oi! Briar!"

Randall heard a "What?" from the back of the workshop, where the tyres were stacked on shelves that reached the roof.

"Fuck off out and get us a sarnie, wouldja?"

"Randall want one too?"

"Nah, he ain't sticking."

"Lazy fuck." Briar's deep, booming voice was cheerful, and soon the eighteen-wheeler of a man strode past the office's window, waving a meaty hand to Randall in passing.

Randall lowered his head in return.

"There we go. Privacy." Preeti dropped back into her chair with a grin. "Spill the beans."

Randall clutched his mug and held it close to his chest, trying to formulate his question in a way that didn't make him sound like a nutter. "I've met someone."

"Ohhh!" Preeti leaned forward, her features lit with salacious glee. "Tell me more!"

"Oh! Not that kind of someone!" He coughed. "Well. Maybe. No. Anyway, look!" He huffed at her. "Right. I mean, I only had this shape on, not my better nose, so I can't swear by it-"

"Out with it!"

"He doesn't have a smell," Randall blurted.

"That's not how the joke goes. You start out with 'my dog has no nose'." She leaned back again and crossed her legs, watching him over her cup.

"Ha ha," he said flatly. "No, but seriously. He doesn't... have a scent. Even when we touched-" he ignored her raised eyebrows "-there wasn't anything. What does that mean?"

"I'd say it means he's some sort of predator."

A laugh escaped him involuntarily, then he swallowed some tea. "Like what? He's not a shifter, right? He'd smell like us."

Preeti flexed her delicate shoulders. "He's not a wolf, certainly. But there are other kinds, so maybe there's some sort out there which masks its scent so it can hunt better." Her eyes widened. "Of course, the only thing to mask your scent from is a creature which relies on smell, so maybe it feeds on werewolves!"

"You suck."

Preeti waggled her eyebrows, then turned serious again. "Maybe you should put your good nose on and take a whiff. See whether he really has no smell whatsoever, or if it's just too faint for humans to detect."

"I'm going to be working with him for a couple of weeks, so I'll see if I can get him to hand me something I can sniff later on."

"Good idea. Get a business card or something. Or just steal his hankie." She gnawed the inside of her cheek a little, then added "Why did you laugh when I said he was some sort of predator?"

"Well, uh." Randall hesitated. "God, I'm going to sound like a right arse. He's blind."

"Oh!" Preeti grinned. "You've discovered the elusive mole-shifter! Imagine the size of his molehills!"

Randall groaned.

"Thanks. I'll be here all week. Try the veal." She tipped her head in a playful nod. "But seriously, you're a dog trainer, so I assume he's got a dog he wants trained, yeah?"

"Yeah."

"Got no smell, has a dog, blind." She finished her mug while she squinted into the middle distance, then shook her head. "Nah, I got nothing. Maybe some kind of underground critter? But they don't need to mask their scent. So maybe he's something that hunts by laying traps and doesn't need eyesight at all."

Randall shuddered. "What, like a spider or something?"

"Sure. Why not?"

"Fuckin' 'ell," he grunted. "What would he turn into? One gigantic spider, or a thousand normal-sized ones?" Neither image appealed to him. "And what about the half-way point? Like some... giant half-man half-spider with eight legs and ten feet tall-" He broke off. "Shit, I'm never going to sleep again."

"My work here is done," Preeti crowed.

"What the hell, Preeti. That's horrible! You can't do that to me!"

"Yeah, but just think of the amount of flies he could get through!" She was enjoying this!

"Well, I'd better look into it, then," Randall muttered, thoroughly put off now.

"If you get stuck in a giant web, call me."

SEVEN

THERE HAD BEEN a couple of events at the gallery since Ellis had last seen Randall, and both of them had carried on way past midnight. Thankfully Han came to one of them, so Ellis didn't feel quite so rotten about it, but now that the weekend was over it was back to the normal routine.

He usually woke mid-afternoon. His alarm was set for four p.m., but today he'd stirred a few minutes earlier, and listened to Tiberius' eagerly thudding tail while he pretended to still be asleep.

It was nice to have someone to wake up to, even if that someone was hairy and wanted to pester him for food.

After he'd fed Tiberius and had a shower, the rest of his evening was occupied with routine. He showered and dressed. He checked his texts and emails, and answered those which required his attention. It was an awful lot like being a caged animal.

Once his phone trilled that sunset had passed, Ellis finally left the flat and walked Tiberius to Green Park. Just about every other park in Mayfair closed at or just after sunset, but Green Park was only a ten minute walk. He gave Tiberius the order to do his toilet business, then set off on a prescribed, memorised route around the vast green.

This was Tiberius' only real exercise time. Ellis often wondered whether the dog might appreciate more, but he seemed happy, and the Mobility Instructor assured him that working all day was every bit as stimulating as merely running around a park would be. It didn't really stop Ellis feeling sorry for the poor bugger, though.

The dog had seemed a little more clingy lately. Maybe he was sliding graciously into middle age, or at least coming to terms with working nights. More likely it was that, on some level, he knew that Ellis had brought a dog trainer in, and had decided to be on his best behaviour.

He heard the snapping of a camera, and he was instantly alert. He tipped his head away from the noise and hunkered down into his coat collar while praying that the tourists were shooting toward the Palace instead of in his direction. What were they doing taking pictures after dark anyway? It *had* to be of the Palace, or of the Victoria Memorial just outside it. Wasn't the Memorial lit up at night, too, or was that only during the more touristy seasons?

Tiberius growled.

Ellis grew uneasy. "Tiberius, no."

The dog wouldn't stop growling. Worse, footsteps drew closer. Other people in the park. What if they were the tourists? What if they had seen Ellis didn't show up on their cameras? Goddamn digital photography. Gone were the days when a vampire could go home safe in the knowledge that a photograph wouldn't get developed for another month or two.

"Hey," came a gentle call from the direction of the feet. "How are you tonight?"

Ellis couldn't put his finger on why the voice sounded familiar. "I'm fine, thanks," he answered, wary.

"That's good. I take it your friend found you after all the other night, yes?"

"Oh!" Ellis ran a palm over his stubble and nodded. "Yes. Thank you. Aye, he showed up. That was St. James' Park, wasn't it?"

"It was." The man's accent was faint, but the more Ellis listened to it the more he thought he could make out an Eastern European rhythm to it.

Tiberius snarled.

"Tiberius, no!" Ellis twitched the harness. "I'm sorry. He isn't usually like this."

"It's okay." The man stopped by Ellis' side. "Don't think I'll try to stroke him, though. Anyway, you look familiar to me. I mean, not just from the other night." He laughed faintly. "I don't think we've met, though. My name is Peter. Peter Barnes."

"Ellis O'Neill." Ellis offered his hand, and Barnes shook it with a tight grip.

"O'Neill. Oh!" Barnes gasped. "Of the O'Neill Gallery?"

Ellis withdrew his hand and smiled briefly. "You've heard of it?"

"Heard of it? It's famous. You're famous! Oh, no wonder I thought that I recognised you!" Barnes' voice still held that undercurrent of tension that Ellis had picked up on the first time they met, but then Tiberius was still expressing himself - if more quietly now. Perhaps Barnes was afraid of dogs, or at the very least of full-sized German Shepherds who growled at him every time they were together.

"Famous?" Ellis shook his head. "It's a minor gallery. I've only been in business for three years. But thank you, it's kind of you to say so."

"Famous," Barnes insisted. "Well, if it is of any help to you, you are in Green Park now."

Ellis laughed and slid his hand over to his watch. "Yeah, when he wants to have his walk he never gets it wrong. Reckon he just wanted an adventure the other night." He brushed his fingers over the ball bearings, then added "I should get back to the gallery, actually. I have an appointment."

"No problem. Would you mind if I were to accompany you that way? I must go to Bond Street for the Central line."

"Oh, well. Of course. Straight on," he added to Tiberius.

Barnes remained to his right, keeping Ellis between himself and the dog as they walked. "There is much work to do this late?"

"It's the art world." Ellis smirked. "Nobody gets out of bed before noon."

"Ha!" Barnes snorted. "I thought to be a painter once. Oh, I am not trying to make contact. Network, as you call it." He laughed. "No. But in my youth I painted and drew. I was not very good."

Ellis' lips twitched. He had yet to meet an artist worth their salt who *thought* they were any good.

"I was not," Barnes insisted as they strolled toward Piccadilly. "But I still enjoy art."

Ellis nodded a little. "I wanted to be an artist when I were a nipper. I wasn't any good at it either, but it took me years to recognise that, so you get kudos for at least knowing when to quit."

Barnes' laugh was touched with bitterness. "Is it easy, to know when to stop?"

"I wouldn't say so." Ellis frowned at the question. It felt oddly personal, as though Barnes were accusing him of something. "What do you mean?"

"Forgive me. I get philosophical at night." Barnes sighed. "Now I work in an office, and so when I walk and think it is the only time I get in which to exercise my imagination. This is a winding route," he added, shifting the subject with ease.

"Oh, I'm sorry." Ellis had been leading Tiberius on his preferred course which veered as far from windows and roads as possible. "Did you want to go another way?"

"No, I am in no particular rush."

Ellis smiled tightly. "I like to go via the tube station and pop down Bolton Street then over to Chesterfield Hill."

"Ah. You like to avoid the busy places?" Barnes chuckled. "Berkeley Street does have many people at this time, doesn't it?"

"Exactly." That and Berkeley Street was riddled with glossy-windowed shops, car showrooms and apartment buildings. It was, to his recollection, like three hundred metres of sheer glass cliff face. "Once you live here a while you start to take the scenic routes everywhere."

"I suppose that is true of all places," Barnes mused.

They walked the rest of the way in companionable chit-chat. Barnes talked about some of his favourite painters and styles, from Precisionism to Neo-Expressionism, Demuth to Hockney. He was certainly able to hold his own, and Ellis allowed his art nerd out to play until Tiberius halted outside the gallery.

"We here already?" Ellis blurted. He offered his hand to Barnes. "Thank you. It's been a pleasure. You're welcome to stop by and come in, you know."

"Perhaps another time?" Barnes laughed. "You did say that you had an appointment to keep."

Ellis swore faintly. "Oh, hell, yes. I have." He fumbled for his watch. "Ah, balls, I'm late. Sorry. I'll have to run off and leave you. But maybe another time?"

"Another time," Barnes agreed.

Ellis proffered his hand, and Barnes shook it with another tight squeeze, and Tiberius' snarl returned.

"I do not think he likes me much at all," Barnes chuckled. "I will see you another time, Mr. O'Neill."

"Ellis, please. Take it easy, Peter."

"You also."

Ellis pushed the door and stepped into the warmth of the gallery, and listened as he closed the door. Three customers. Jay, speaking with them, his absolute best sales pitch in full flow. And Randall, already waiting in his office.

Bugger.

He ran his hand over the door to check that it had closed correctly, then strode toward the stairs, offering a polite smile toward Jay. He heard a smattering of murmured greetings from the customers, but none were voices he recognised, so he continued on to the stairs.

Which was when he noticed that Tiberius had stopped grumbling.

He halted at the bottom step and reached down to pet Tiberius' head. The dog's heartbeat was normal, and he was panting from the walk, heating the air with his breath.

"You're a good boy," Ellis murmured. "A very good boy. What was all that about, eh? Problem with art-lovers? Don't you dare start growling at my customers. No way. You wouldn't do that, would you?" He smiled fondly as he ruffled Tiberius' fluffy ears, and heard the swish of his tail.

At least Randall's visit wouldn't be in vain. There was definitely something up with Tiberius, and Ellis prayed it was something the trainer could help with. There was only one way to find out.

He reached for the handrail and mounted the stairs.

EIGHT

RANDALL HAD ELLIS' office to himself for a few minutes. Jay was with customers downstairs, and Ellis was running late.

The temptation to sniff things was great.

He nursed his tea. Jay had made one this time rather than run to the nearest cafe, so it was in a sturdy ceramic mug with some poppies printed on it. It felt oddly mundane, like it had come from a supermarket. When he finished it he'd have to turn it over and see if there was a logo stamped on the underside. For some reason he'd expected bone china with famous paintings on the sides, but maybe the good china was reserved for shindigs.

He couldn't go around Ellis' desk and put nose to chair. That would be weird. What if they had CCTV in here, or if anyone walked in on him? And they *had* to have CCTV; art galleries were worth a fortune, weren't they? Sooner or later someone could review the footage and find the dog trainer with his nose in the upholstery.

Yeah. They probably wouldn't invite him back after that.

Instead Randall used his time to observe his surroundings from his chair. Training dogs instilled a level of watchfulness which even other shifters often lacked. He had to be constantly on the alert to a dog's mental state, as well as his environment to preempt potential difficulties before they were allowed to adversely affect the dog he was handling. If an animal was afraid of smaller dogs, he had to see smaller dogs coming; if it had a habit of chasing cats, Randall had to be damn sure he knew where all the cats were. It was always better to prevent a situation than to try and derail it once it was in full swing.

The office was neat and spotless. Furniture was limited to two desks, the chairs around each, and then storage units along the walls which left the floor completely clear. He leaned over and peered at the feet of his chair to find that they were perfectly slotted into dents they had made in the short, functional carpet over the years. The empty chair beside him was equally rooted, as were the chairs at Jay's desk. Perhaps people who used the chairs may have occasionally moved them, but for the most part they remained exactly where they were, and got returned to their spot if ever they had been relocated.

Ellis' desk had some keyboard-like device in the centre, in front of a monitor. The device was no longer or wider than a regular computer keyboard, but it sat flat and was around two centimetres thick. A row of metal pins occupied the lower half of the device, and the top had eight completely unmarked black buttons which were ergonomically placed in such a manner to suggest that they were for fingers. Randall leaned closer and realised the metal pins were grouped into blocks of eight, and each block contributed to the row, which spanned the width of the device. A USB cable ran from it and threaded down through a hole in the desk behind the monitor. Could it be some kind of braille reader or keyboard? Or both at the same time, even?

That would be pretty damn awesome. Then why have the monitor? To share information with the sighted, maybe? Or was a monitor bright enough for Ellis' vision to see?

He finished his tea while he continued to look around. The computer had to be stored safely away within the desk. That made sense. Apart from anything else it would stop Tiberius' long hairs getting into the fans.

Randall itched to be able to shift. Just five seconds would give him so much more information. In a private office the scent trails in here could be months old; he would be able to find out how often customers came up here and how many Ellis had; he'd be able to spot a crumb dropped from a pastry even if it had been vacuumed up again within minutes.

He'd be able to tell whether Ellis had any scent whatsoever.

He fidgeted in his chair, then sat upright. He heard the distinctive

43

clikclikclik of claws on a hard surface, and turned toward the door as Ellis and Tiberius reached the top of the stairs.

"Randall," Ellis said as he walked into the room. He offered his right hand in Randall's direction - or, Randall supposed, toward the chairs which rarely moved. "I am so sorry I'm late."

Randall clasped his hand and shook it gently. "It's okay. Tiberius?"

"Eh. Not really?" Ellis sounded doubtful. "He was acting up, but not like that. Just grumbling at people again." He moved around his desk and sat. "Did Jay at least get you a cuppa?"

"Yeah, yeah." Randall tapped his fingernails against the mug he still held. "All good."

"Great. Right. Where do we start?"

"Okay." Randall leaned forward in his seat. "What I want to do is spend this week reiterating his Guide Dog training. Go completely back to basics and test him on every command he knows. We'll reward him at every single correctly-performed manoeuvre and heap praise on him like he's still a puppy."

Ellis pursed his lips, but said nothing.

Randall couldn't help but smile at that. "You can interrupt at any time."

"You're the expert," Ellis insisted.

"And you're the customer."

Ellis ran one hand across his desk's surface, then said "He does receive praise for his work. It's how Guide Dogs are managed; they can't have treats - it teaches them to seek food and they can't be distracted by discarded wrappers or dropped snacks."

Randall grinned. "You're spot on. Which is good. It's not easy to work with people who won't do as they're instructed or listen to the reasons they're given. Training a dog's only one half of the equation; if the owner doesn't keep it up then all the work's for nothing." He watched Ellis' hand as it idly felt for the corner of his braille keyboard, as though the gallery owner were assuring himself it was there. "With that said, I'm sure you know all about Intelligent Disobedience, yeah?"

Ellis' fingers withdrew to his lap and his head lifted. "Aye. Tiberius has to overrule me if I give him an order which could put us both in danger. He's very bright."

"He is. And I'm really wondering whether what he's doing when he takes you off-route is exactly that: protecting you from something he perceives as a threat."

Ellis' brows lowered, and he pursed his lips into a frown. "You reckon so?"

"It would explain why he only does it sporadically, so for tonight I suggest that we work out what along your regular routes might be giving him cause for concern. If we go do your most common route we can check it out, see what he reacts to."

"My most common route would be between here and home." Ellis sounded uncertain.

Was he nervous about allowing Randall to find out where he lived? That would certainly fit in with Preeti's theory that Ellis was a predator of some kind. No instinct in the world would convince Randall to take something into his home which wasn't fully trustworthy or already dead. And what if he were some kind of spider shifter? Would his home be filled with dangerous webbing, ready to ensnare those willing to follow him in over the threshold?

"Uh." Randall cleared his throat. "We don't have to go all the way to your door. I'm guessing most of his misdirections don't happen within a few feet of home, am I right?"

"Correct." Ellis certainly seemed relieved now.

"Okay then." Randall stood and took his mug to the sink, and washed it as thoroughly as he could, then dried his hands on a nearby tea towel. "Take me whenever you're ready."

His cheeks flared the moment the words were past his lips, and Ellis laughed softly. "Well, you're forward. But I thought we could wait until the issues with Tiberius were resolved."

"Uhhh. Ummm. Err." Randall felt like he'd stalled. His brain refused to supply the words, so his mouth was left defending the Western Front all on its own. "That's not what I meant," he blurted.

Ellis just gave a decidedly dirty little smile as he steered Tiberius toward the door, and Randall found himself hurrying along at Ellis' heel.

They left quietly past Jay still selling his heart out to the customers present, and stepped into the cold night air. Ellis directed Tiberius along the Mews, and began a winding route through side-streets and alleyways.

Randall didn't wish to leap to conclusions but it struck him that if he had lost his sight he might not want to walk down London's alleyways at night. Mind you, he was an East End boy, Spitalfields born and raised. Even when he moved out he didn't go far; his business and home were in Stepney, just down the road from the rest of his family. They were pretty safe areas now, but hadn't been so pretty when he was a kid.

Was Ellis attempting to mislead him? Make up some route on the spot and take Randall far away from his own, real home? That would be pretty elaborate, wouldn't it?

He watched Tiberius as they walked. The dog was patient and attentive. He knew where he was going.

This was their regular route, or at least one of them.

Randall looked around them in between checking Tiberius' body language. He looked to objects overhead: streetlamps; shop signs. He paid attention to parked cars and shuttered garages alike. The pavement was mostly even, but where it wasn't Tiberius walked Ellis around the cracks and bumps without any doubts.

They were a team. There wasn't a damn thing wrong with Tiberius.

Something niggled at Randall, though. They still chose small Mews and quiet streets over faster thoroughfares. Hadn't Ellis said that the purpose of a dog was to save transit time? Then why the snakelike path?

"He seems to be doing well," Randall murmured.

Ellis chuckled. "Aye, little git." There was pure affection in those words. "I'm telling you, it's because you're watching him."

"Could be. Could be." Randall glanced away again and caught his own reflection in the window of a parked car. Nothing untoward there.

What the hell was still nagging at him, scratching away at the back of his thoughts like a rat digging through a box?

A couple of minutes went by before they passed another window. Cars were few and far between, and whatever houses they passed were set back from the pavement with raised windows and railings to stop people falling into their basement access. Randall's reflection looked back at him, every bit as perplexed as he felt.

Shouldn't Ellis have a reflection too?

Randall bit his lip. At their pace the window was soon behind them, and he found himself scouring ahead for other reflective surfaces. There weren't a huge number to be found.

Ellis' route avoided major roads with their big shiny street-level windows.

What did any of that even mean? What kind of thing didn't smell and didn't have a reflection? How was it even *possible* to not have a reflection, anyway? Randall hadn't exactly stormed through his Physics GCSE with flying colours, but he was fairly sure all light travelled in a straight line. It didn't bounce off something then just disappear.

"Are you all right?" Ellis spoke softly.

"Uh." Randall shoved his hands into his pockets and tried not to panic. "Just, um. Trying to work out what Tiberius might be reacting to. He's been fine this whole time, so I'm starting to think maybe it could be people or a specific type of person he's having trouble with."

"Such as?"

"People who are behaving erratically. Drunks, tourists, drug addicts. Maybe he's not sure about people who are diabetic, or have cancer; he might think those things are dangerous to you."

Ellis' thin eyebrows climbed above his frames. "I'd heard dogs could detect disease. Do you think that might be what he's doing?"

"Could be. Or, like I say, people behaving in a manner he finds threatening."

Ellis chuckled at that. "This is Mayfair. The worst he's going to encounter is the occasional posh fella rolling out of the Lansdowne Club." He hesitated, and his look became pensive. "Though when he misbehaved earlier there *was* someone nearby with a camera."

"You heard it?"

Ellis nodded. "SLR. Very distinctive. Very loud."

"That's one of the big cameras, right?"

"It is."

Randall sucked air through his teeth. "Maybe it's tourists, then. They do behave unpredictably. They stop without warning, wave books or maps around, approach strangers, take pictures of things. Maybe that's what's setting him off. I'll come up with some exercises to try and acclimatise him to that kind of behaviour."

"That would be great." Ellis smiled gently. "I worry that someone's going to take offence over the way he snarls at them."

"He's a big lad," Randall agreed. "But we'll work it out. He wouldn't have passed his training and been partnered with you if he wasn't damn good at his job. Shall we head back toward the gallery?"

"Absolutely." Ellis turned Tiberius around, pausing to fuss his ears.

Randall walked the whole way with him and discussed how they could perhaps borrow Jay to help pretend to be a tourist and test their theory.

It was a good theory. Fairly sound, with a few minor holes.

But it didn't even begin to explain how the hell Ellis didn't show up in what few windows they passed on the way.

NINE

THE ATMOSPHERE within the gallery had changed. Gone were the chatting customers and the sound of Jay attempting to make a sale. Instead Ellis could detect a whiff of alcohol, and two heartbeats thundering along almost in sync with one-another.

Ellis pushed the door closed as loudly as he could, then called "Jay? Are you in?"

He heard a rush of breath and the rustle of cloth against skin, and he covered his mouth with his hand to try and prevent his laugh from getting out and causing havoc.

"Upstairs!" Jay called, sounding flustered.

Ellis rubbed his stubble in an attempt to make his face behave, then headed up to his office.

Han's cologne was distinctive. He favoured a reasonably popular one, but the manner with which it interacted with his skin was unique to him. Still, Ellis couldn't rush over to give his favourite customer a hug without at least pretending that he didn't know who was in his office.

"Are you drinking up here?" he said as he stepped in.

Han laughed. "I'm sorry. I brought a bottle of bubbly over. Would you like some?"

"Han!" Ellis smiled broadly and held his arms out for a hug. "Did I interrupt? Don't tell me London is all out of classy locations to seduce your husband in! Is my office all you could find?"

Han stepped in and returned the hug tightly. Ellis heard Jay hiccup with embarrassment. "Just as well you got back," Han said cheerfully. "I was about to grease him up and go at it over his desk!"

"Han!" Jay sounded horrified. "Oh my god! You are so dirty!"

"You love it!"

Ellis patted Han's back and stepped away, his laughter finally allowed to roam free. "You don't get any better. Have you come to collect your man?"

"Actually, I came to see you."

Ellis sat at his desk and heard a faint bump as Han drew a chair out of its carpet-grooves. He was one of the few people who would move his chairs, but at least Han always put them back once he was done with them.

"Me?" He released Tiberius' harness and undid the buttons of his jacket. "You're opening a second office and desperately need twenty paintings?"

"I wish. That'd be amazing. Would you like some bubbly?"

Ellis narrowed his eyes. "You're up to something."

"He won't tell me what it is," Jay said as he sat in the other chair. "He's being all secretive."

Ellis faked a gasp. "Han! He's your husband! How could you keep secrets from him?"

"Hey. You don't get where I am today by showing your whole hand at once," Han said dryly. "But yes. Can't ever fool you, Ellis. I've got a favour to ask."

"Anything." Ellis spoke without hesitation.

Han had been a loyal customer since The O'Neill Gallery was just a room above another shop over in Fitzrovia which showcased a handful of unknown artists. He'd said once that he felt that since his own business was a newborn, it felt right to work with an art dealer whose business was equally unheard-of. Ellis owed a great deal of his gallery's success to Han's early patronage, but Han never expected favours or sought a discount. Even better, when he brought guests to the gallery or even just attended events for the fun of it, he would leap in with enthusiasm to translate for the gallery's Chinese customers; although his own family spoke Cantonese, Han had busted a gut to learn Mandarin long before he began writing iPhone games.

Ellis owed Han a hell of a lot.

"I need Jay."

Jay gulped down a mouthful of champagne.

"Need, as in-" Ellis left it hanging for Han to fill in.

"I have an overseas business trip in a few days. An Expo in Paris. I know it's short notice, but I'd appreciate if Jay could have some time off and come with me."

It felt as though this were a test. Was Han finally reaching his limit over all the late nights? Or was it really so simple as a romantic getaway wrapped around a software show? "We have a couple of events this weekend," Ellis said, uncertain.

"I'll find you a temp. I'll *pay* for the temp."

The thought of losing Jay for a few days was terrifying. Of course he couldn't expect Jay to be at his side 24/7; that was unreasonable. The man had his own life. Hell, Han had introduced Jay to him in the first place.

Ellis had poached Han's personal assistant, for crying out loud. After all the support Han had given him, Jay had handed in his notice and come to work in a minor art gallery instead of by his husband's side.

This was an opportunity, Ellis told himself. A chance for him to try and break his dependence on Jay's constant, kindly presence. A chance to give back to Han what he'd unwittingly pinched two years back. He hadn't meant to just nick Han's staff; it had been Jay's idea.

Sweet Jay. He deserved Han, he really did. And he bloody well deserved a trip to Paris.

Ellis nodded slowly. "You don't have to do that. Of course Jay can have the time off." He put as much honesty as he could into his smile. "Take him away and show him the sights."

"I'll source a temp. No arguments. Once we're back we'll see about getting you another member of staff here, too. The gallery's growing. Hire some people, Ellis. Stop working into the early hours all the time."

Ellis laughed weakly. Han couldn't ever know why exactly he worked so late. He didn't like the idea of allowing more people into his life to observe his odd hours.

"We're really going to Paris?" Jay was incredulous, and Ellis gave thanks for his interruption.

"Yeah. You're passport's in date, right?" Han chuckled.

"Oh, shit, don't do that to me!"

Ellis heard a pat of skin against fabric.

"Come to Paris and I promise to do what I like to you!"

"Filthy beast!" Jay's odour shifted with his arousal, though.

"Hey. None of that in my office. You're both reprehensible. Get out." Ellis laughed.

"I know I am," Han replied.

"Oh, quick question," Ellis added. "Jay, those customers earlier. They buy anything?"

He knew the answer before Jay said a word. The way Jay took a breath, the sound of his body shifting as his posture changed. "No," Jay said slowly. "They were here almost an hour, but in the end, nothing."

Ellis turned toward Han. "This temp of yours better be a good salesman."

Jay gasped, feigning hurt. "You wouldn't replace me! I'm too adorable!"

"You're a *bit* adorable, it's true."

Han laughed. "I'll see what I can find. Thank you, Ellis. This means a lot to me."

Ellis' smile returned, more open and genuine this time. "You two mean a hell of a lot to me, Han. Go on, take him home and treat him like a prince."

"You betcha."

After they had gone, the gallery was quiet but for the noises most people wouldn't be able to hear. Tiberius' heartbeat, the fizz of champagne, the high-pitched buzz from the electronics scattered around. Without customers, without his computer on, if he really listened he could hear beyond his walls: the tenants in the apartments above his gallery; distant cars; indistinguishable chatter.

All his concentration earned him was an intense sense of how utterly lonely his existence truly was.

He tugged his sunglasses off and rubbed his eyes. The office was bright enough that his world turned grey, and he hated it. He hated the taunting from his eyes, the fading remains of sight that couldn't be saved and now which would never deteriorate the rest of the way.

The blindness he'd tried to prepare himself for wouldn't quite come, yet he couldn't see well enough in the dark to live the life Jonas had planned for him.

What kind of asshole turns a blind man, anyway?

Oh, Jonas had said he never realised Ellis was blind, sure. But Jonas *had* been full of shit. He'd claimed to be five centuries old and plagued with the ineffable *ennui* of eternal life, but Ellis had found out after Jonas' death that the idiot only got turned in 1999, stoned off his tits at a rave in a warehouse.

Maybe that had been Jonas' problem. Ellis couldn't even shave without it regrowing within moments; his eyes were frozen at the stage of degeneration they'd already reached. Everything about his body had been preserved at the moment he was turned, like he'd been pickled for posterity.

What if Jonas had been pickled into a state of permanent high?

It could explain a lot. It'd stand to reason that Jonas hadn't thought that a guy with sunglasses and a guide dog could be blind if Jonas had been a total space cadet every waking hour. It'd certainly explain why Jonas' power had been some kind of universal understanding of language, if Ellis wanted to take a full hippie approach to this train of thought. It might even explain the fight.

Jesus, the fight.

Jonas spent those early nights looking after Ellis. He fetched willing girls for Ellis to learn how to feed, he taught Ellis about the Council and their laws. He was even the one to suggest that Ellis try braille again now that his senses "worked better". And then Jonas' interest just drifted off like a drunk in the night. He stopped trying to help. He started to spin increasingly wild stories about London in its "heyday" - whether that was the 19th century or earlier changed regularly. He accused Ellis of faking blindness.

Everything went downhill from there, fast. There had been bitter words. Then Jonas came to the gallery one night reeking of blood, and he'd threatened to kill Jay.

Jay never knew. He wasn't working that night. The gallery was empty, with Ellis and Tiberius in the office. The door had been unlocked; nobody wandered down a Mews late at night then randomly tried art gallery doors unless they meant to go inside. Ellis had smelled the blood from his office and shut Tiberius in there to go handle Jonas. Damned if he was going to allow the threats to move onto his dog, too, and the blood was enough for Ellis to estimate Jonas' location.

He'd gone downstairs to face Jonas, and Jonas had screamed that he was sick of Ellis leeching off him.

He'd come to destroy Ellis.

It wasn't against the Laws. Vampires destroying each other didn't happen often, but if it came about over a territory dispute it was generally brushed off as one of those things. Jonas didn't want Ellis' meagre territory. He just seemed to have gone insane, and Ellis was the easiest target going.

Other than whoever's blood Jonas was wearing.

Jonas attacked him, and Ellis defended himself. And it had been Ellis who won. He'd used dirty, illegal tactics and they'd saved his arse.

When the Constable came to investigate, Ellis cradled his lie within the truth. The ash remains of a destroyed vampire told no tales, and Jonas had smeared human blood around the place in the scuffle, which lent credence to Ellis' story of a pitched struggle. There was no reason for the Constable to believe anything other than Ellis' story that he'd fought for his life and battered Jonas' head against the floor until there was nothing left of him.

Jonas came into his territory and attacked him, and Ellis was within his right to defend himself to the death, and that was that.

And Ellis absolutely didn't mention that he'd drunk Jonas dry.

What the hell else could he do? He couldn't see his opponent. He wasn't a brawler. Jonas was damn well going to destroy him, and then probably go right up to his office and eat Tiberius to regain his strength.

Ellis had taken the gamble that a vampire's bite would paralyse another vampire as readily as it did anything living, and it had paid off.

He'd broken a law that carried a death sentence. Death by feeding was strictly forbidden. It was seen as gross, indecent; an act of perverts and the insane.

But god damn it, Ellis was alive now, and he bloody well intended to stay that way, alone or not.

He reached for his glasses and slid them on, then reached down to the constant companion he'd risked his whole existence for.

"C'mon, you great hairy lummox," he murmured to Tiberius. "Let's go home."

Tiberius stood, patient as an ox, ready to get to work.

TEN

PREETI'S OFFICE had gained a car exhaust, propped against a filing cabinet. Randall didn't think the muffler was supposed to hang off it like that, but maybe Preeti intended to fix it.

He wasn't interested enough to ask.

"Right. Briar's going to be made of sandwiches by the end of the week." Preeti came back into her office, and set about making tea. "You could just talk about stuff in front of him, you know?"

"I dunno. He's kinda massive and terrifying-"

Preeti's thick ponytail fell over her shoulder as she threw her head back and laughed raucously. The sound was vast compared to her petite frame. "He's a teddy bear!"

Randall didn't argue. That was his place in the pack: to cower and not argue. He waited for the tea and thanked her for it.

"So, is it a werespider?" she asked as she sat.

"I dunno." Randall shuffled back in his chair. "But I've found something else."

"Well? Don't keep me hanging, Rand, this ain't a game show."

He filled his lungs and held his breath a second. This was ridiculous. It was impossible.

People who turned into wolves were pretty impossible too, though.

"He hasn't got a reflection," he exhaled.

She stared at him. "Like, what. A vampire?"

Randall gulped a mouthful of tea, and burned the roof of his mouth in the process. "Ow. Balls. Yeah, like a vampire. Maybe?"

Preeti crossed her legs and waggled one steel-toed boot in the air while she blew on her tea. "Right, well. He doesn't smell and he doesn't reflect. That's super predatory behaviour, right? The lack of smell on its own could be a defensive strategy, but not reflecting suggests maybe a creature that wants to cut down its chances of being seen in the peripheral vision of its prey, right?"

Randall nodded slowly. "I'd say so. That makes some sort of sense. Assuming that these things are evolved traits, but evolution takes millions of years, and there weren't so many mirrors or sheets of glass around in the Jurassic Era."

"Okay, selective breeding, then. Like dogs. You know dogs. How long did it take to breed a thousand totally different dog breeds out of a few wolves, eh?"

"Er." Randall squinted. "Humans have been domesticating animals for, ah, thousands of years."

"Which is way shorter than it would take for dogs to evolve from wolves."

"Well, they probably wouldn't of their own accord-"

"Because there's no evolutionary requirement to get cute and obedient, right." Preeti finally sipped.

Randall eyeballed his mug, trying to decide whether another sip right now would just cause pain. "Right."

"Then maybe it's not evolved, or bred. Maybe it's a curse."

He took the risk, and thanked his shifter physiology. The burn had already healed up nicely. "At the risk of asking a stupid question, how would that even be done?"

Preeti shrugged. "A god, a wizard, I dunno. Maybe some warlock got attacked by a vampire once and made a spell that would warn future generations that these things weren't human? Maybe they just don't smell, but he made them unable to cast a reflection too? I mean, once we get to the Middle Ages glass was a thing, especially in churches. Maybe *that's* why vampires can't go in churches? It's got nothing to do with holy ground or whatever: it's because churches have shiny surfaces in them and it made it easy for villagers to spot the predator in their midst."

"That's-" Randall blinked. "That kinda makes a lot of sense."

"I mean, we're presupposing a lot of shit here," Preeti added. "Briar might know more. I'll ask him. Really, though, you should ask him yourself. You *are* part of the pack, Rand. We need you as much as you need us."

"It doesn't feel like I'm needed."

He hadn't meant it to come out like that. Not so easily, or so brutal in tone. It wasn't a whine, he wasn't complaining, but his words rang with truth.

They sat in silence a while, both drinking their tea.

"What's this about?" Preeti plonked her mug on the table.

Randall fidgeted with his mug. He ran his thumb over a chip and explored it with his nail. "The pack doesn't need me. And I'm getting tired of being shat on by people who think it's okay just because they've decided I'm the Omega."

"You *are* the Omega."

"That's bollocks, Preeti. The whole Omega theory is bollocks. It came about through observation of captive wolves taken from several different packs. They weren't a family unit, and they didn't behave naturally. They all fought for dominance 'cause there was a whole bunch of young adult males in the sample pool, and in the wild they would've either stayed with their families or wandered off to form new packs with some nice lady wolf they picked up along the way. Wolf packs are biological families. You get like two or three generations of children from the same parents. *That* is a pack. They don't beat on the little guy for shits and giggles. They don't *have* an Omega. And all this 'pick on Randall because Omegas are totally a thing' feels downright fucking racist."

Preeti blinked at him. "Er. Only half of us are white."

"Oh, come on." Randall crossed his arms and scowled. "I'm the only black guy. You're shagging Briar, so you get a pass. And Nazim's just as eager to put the boot in as everyone else. Fuck, Preeti, do you have *any* idea what my mum would say if she saw me bowing and scraping to a white bloke? This is the 21st century! It goes too far. It's bullying, and I'm getting sick of it."

Her eyes narrowed slowly, and she cracked her knuckles, then dropped her booted foot to the floor. In a calm, level voice she said, "The full moon's near, Rand. You're just getting moonsick, that's all. This is why you need us. This is what Alphas do. Briar helps us stay on the level, keep our heads. Rand, I helped you when you were about to turn, didn't I?"

Randall chewed the inside of his cheek. "Yeah. Yeah, you did."

"You would have gone home to your family and changed in a tiny flat with a single mum and an older brother, and you probably would have torn them to pieces. Maybe even eaten them. But we found you first, right?"

Randall's gaze slid away toward the broken muffler. "Yeah. Preeti, I don't want to sound ungrateful. There's no way mum or Kieran would be alive if it weren't for you."

"And we love you. You're part of our family now." She sighed a little. "Come with me. Come on. Let's round them up and we can all talk."

Randall fidgeted some more, but Preeti's gaze fixed him in his seat. She wasn't going to let this go.

"Okay." His shoulders sagged.

Suddenly hanging out with a vampire seemed way more fun than it should be.

PREETI PHONED BRIAR. Randall didn't know where this alleged "sandwich shop" was but Briar still hadn't returned from it an hour after he got sent away.

The pack had territory all over the East End. They roamed from Whitechapel to the Hackney Marshes, and sometimes as far as East Ham. There were other packs beyond, in Essex or south of the Thames, but really they had the north side of the river to themselves so far as they could tell. They mostly chose to avoid the posh spots out of lack of interest.

When they all got together, though, they went underground. Whitechapel had a long-abandoned tube station beneath the street which Nazim had managed to get a key to, and he'd made copies for each of them. They couldn't spend too long down there, since London Underground staff also had keys and sometimes came down for whatever reason, but for the most part it was a useful location hidden from prying eyes.

St. Mary's station had been bombed into oblivion during the Blitz until the only use left for it was as an air raid shelter, so now the old ticket hall was bricked up and ancient staircases removed. Platform access was behind another door, but that door remained shut; the lines that ran through the platforms were still in use, and trains frequently rumbled through the deserted station with most passengers none the wiser that it was even out there in the blackness.

By the time Preeti let herself and Randall in through the discreet little doorway set back from Whitechapel Road, he could smell wolves. It was too soon to identify who, especially as there was a pile of rotting vegetables stacked near the doorway, presumably abandoned by market traders.

Preeti closed and locked the door, and they hurried down the narrow, poorly-lit stairs with Preeti in the lead.

At the bottom of the stairs was a small room, with crooked iron railings halfway across it and the ghost of an old staircase embedded in the walls on either side. The station had been bricked up in a piecemeal fashion, so the walls were patchwork. Now and then remains of the original bricks could be seen, old and with rotted mortar powdered between them. The newer bricks were hardly recent, though, mottled with lichen and damp. Preeti led them around the battered railings and to a small, simple plywood door.

Randall heard them before he saw them; yips and grumbles, paws and claws that clattered on the concrete floor. Preeti pulled the door open and revealed a scattered pile of clothes on the other side, and once they were through she shifted the moment she'd closed the door. Her skin rippled, and like waves cascading across her body each ripple became crested with spines of fur which unfurled and fluffed out as her whole shape buckled and twisted.

It took two or three seconds at most. Before her clothes had even finished sloughing from her lithe body, Preeti was on four paws, shaking her way out of her overalls. Her t-shirt hung around her, trapped by her forelegs, and Randall crouched to help her out of it.

She was a small figure even in her wolf form. Her fur was not as long as that of most of the others in the pack, and was a pretty reddish-grey. Briar sometimes called her "Coyote", but she was definitely a wolf. Nazim's wolf form was similarly small, but his fur was more shot through with white patches. Randall suspected that they both took lineage from the Indian wolf, but he couldn't even begin to think of what that meant for the history of wolf shifters. Was the shifter originally one species which then interbred with wolves over the millennia? Had they spread across the world as humans had, or even alongside them?

These weren't questions anyone Randall spoke with ever had the answers to. Worse, nobody seemed to care to find the answers. It wasn't in a wolf's nature to be introspective or wonder about the past; they cared about the present, and it seemed to be their human side which allowed them to plan for the future too.

Was this why they were so scattered now? Was this the shifter survival plan, to intermingle with the humans while those humans consumed the last wildernesses? Had the eradication of wolves in the Renaissance also seen widespread extermination of shifters? It would explain why shifters were born to human parents.

His species had become a recessive gene that had to be present in both parents, and even then chances seemed slim. Kieran wasn't a shifter, and neither was his mum. They had the same dad, before he ran off with some tart from Essex and left them all behind, so that was as far as Randall's theory could really go. He wasn't a geneticist; he trained dogs for a living.

He sighed as Nazim ran over and nipped his forearm.

"Miles away," he explained to the boisterous wolf.

Nazim flattened his ears and fluffed up his tail, then showed his teeth. It was an aggressive demand for play, and it was what Randall had hoped not to get into at all today.

"Okay. Give me a second."

Nazim snorted and backed off to wait, so Randall peeled his shirt off over his head and put it on the pile, then tidied the pile somewhat. It was a delaying tactic, and he saw Nazim's ears swivel in annoyance.

Randall loosened his bootlaces and pulled the boots off, then began his shift.

It wasn't comfortable, but it didn't hurt. Shifting was like a sneezing fit, or being tickled. The discomfort came from his body twisting and twitching beyond his direct control.

Every muscle clenched and spasmed as the change tore through him. Ripples of fur broke out while his bones and muscles reshaped themselves until he couldn't stand on two legs anymore. By the time he had fallen forward, his hands were paws, and he landed with ease.

His field of view narrowed, yet his peripheral vision became far greater than his human sight. Colours became muted as red and green disappeared from his world, replaced by high-definition greys. It mattered little down here, though; the light was so poor that his wolf eyes saw far more precisely than his human ones could, and the miasma of scent pools and trails were colourful in their own way.

Nazim barely waited for Randall to step free of his jeans before he lunged in to nip and taunt Randall's flank. Randall could smell Preeti now, as well as Jim and Lara.

Briar's scent was a week old. He wasn't here yet.

Randall yelped as Nazim tugged on a mouthful of fur, and sank down so that he could roll and show his belly.

They were being rough. Preeti bounced toward him now, with Jim and Laura in tow.

Jesus fuck, where was Briar?

The full moon was coming, and the pack had assembled without their Alpha to keep them calm. And now their favourite toy had arrived.

Randall could heal torn tufts of fur. He would patch up fast after bruises and scrapes. But the teeth and claws of his own kind were as terrifying as silver itself. Without Briar there to stop them they could get out of hand and bite.

And if they got *really* out of hand they might change to a more deadly shape.

Randall concentrated on appearing submissive. He curled his spine and drew his tail between his hind legs, and made sure he didn't make eye contact with any of them as they piled in to bully him in between snapping and snarling at one another.

He hated it. Every behaviour he worked hard at teaching dogs to overcome ran riot among his pack. They were like a bunch of children, none of them willing to take responsibility for their own actions, always willing to fall back on the tired old excuse "this is how a pack works".

Jim's posture shifted. His ears came forward and his fur stood on end as he showed Randall his teeth and snarled.

Then Nazim joined in.

Oh shit.

Had he let himself get angry? Had he missed a cue? Was he so tied up in his thoughts that he had failed to show deference at the right moment?

"That's enough."

Briar's voice was a lifeline, but Randall didn't dare turn toward it. He heard it as the door opened and the massive man entered the old air raid shelter, but he remained in place, his chest heaving as he clung to Briar's words and prayed that the others did the same.

Nazim's ears flicked slightly.

"Let it go. Mother Luna is almost full, but we are a pack. We are strongest together. Back down."

The wolves around him relaxed. Their hackles slowly sank, and their tails lowered.

This had to be some sort of survival thing, like the way a mother could recognise her own baby's cries among several others. There was something about Briar's words which bypassed the anger, the broiling rage of the moon's lingering presence, and soothed it into slumber. A pack without an Alpha would tear itself asunder the moment someone made a minute misstep during the full moon, of that Randall had no doubt.

"Let's talk."

The wolves slunk away from Randall, and he lay on his back until he was sure he could move. He rolled slowly onto his side, then onto his front, and kept his head down throughout.

Most of the pack had already shifted by the time he dared look at them. Preeti stood by Briar's side, naked where her husband was fully clothed. Jim had changed too, shivering in the chill of the room, his human body six feet tall and lean like a weasel's. Lara shifted and pushed herself to stand.

Nazim eyed Randall, then he too took his human shape, tall and broad and with a long scar along his left thigh.

Now that he was in no danger, Randall shifted and pushed away from the cold ground once his human skin was in direct contact with it. Skin tones became visible, instead of the washed out miasma of grey and yellow his wolf eyes saw. Lara was the palest of them, her skin white-pink in a tone Jim called "English Rose". Jim's colouring was warmer, but still white. Nazim was a leathered brown, his Bangladeshi heritage lending him a warm skin tone with glossy black hair that he kept short. Preeti's brown, by contrast, was cooler and paler, and her hair bore the faintest hints of red.

Briar towered over them all. White, tanned from near-constant outdoor work, with ruddy-brown hair and eyes like sapphires, he was as close as Randall thought he'd ever come to meeting a bear. He was massive by human standards: six foot five, with shoulders so broad he had to enter most rooms sideways. How the hell he found shoes big enough was anyone's guess.

Briar gathered them all together and the pack pulled clothes on. Now that they had been calmed by their Alpha their play was more relaxed, although Randall received a shove while he tried to pull his jeans on that almost toppled him.

"Randall's met someone," Preeti said as people began to sit in a circle.

Jim jeered and nudged Randall's shoulder. "You dog!"

"Not *that* kind of someone," Randall mumbled as he sat.

"Better not be, anyway," Preeti said, her voice gaining an edge. "He's not human, or a wolf."

Briar looked over at Randall. "Then what is he?"

"We, um." Randall's throat tightened. "We think he might be a vampire."

Jim snorted, and Nazim sniggered into his hand.

"Why do you think that?" Briar turned to Preeti.

"He doesn't have a smell, and he doesn't have a reflection. He makes his appointments with Randall at night."

"To train a dog?"

"Yes."

Briar asked Randall, "Is training dogs at night normal?"

"Not really. Dogs have a very strong internal body clock. They like to be asleep at night and awake in the day, unless their owner's also nocturnal."

"And this dog's alert and attentive for training?"

Randall nodded. "Yeah. He's well used to being awake late into the evening, at least."

Briar's gaze swept toward the walls while he thought, and the pack watched him and waited. "Find out what he is," he finally ordered, his blue eyes returning to Randall. "Don't get attached until we have the answer. You must understand that if it is a vampire, I won't tolerate its existence."

Randall blinked quickly. "Can I ask why not?"

"I won't have fleas, Rand. You get too many on a dog and the dog will die. I love London, and if it's got fleas, I want them destroyed." Briar leaned toward him, and Randall's insides clenched. "Find out what he is. If he's a vampire, kill it."

"What if it-" Randall cursed himself "-he isn't?"

"Then we'll cross that bridge when we come to it, won't we?"

Randall felt sick. He wasn't a killer, and Ellis wasn't a flea. His Alpha had ordered him to murder a walking, talking, intelligent creature.

"I-" He fumbled for his phone and feigned checking the time, but it could've said four in the afternoon and he wouldn't have given a shit. "I have an appointment. I gotta go."

"Let us know what happens, either way." Briar's words were a command, not a request.

"Yeah." Randall stood and backed toward the door, then hurried out without looking back.

ELEVEN

ELLIS FOUND pleasure in Randall's company. The man was always on time, always thoughtful and patient, and Tiberius responded well to him. In Ellis' experience, Tiberius only trusted decent people.

The week had begun with frustration, but it took only a couple of evenings for Ellis to eagerly anticipate the appointments. Was that silly? He couldn't really have any feelings for Randall, could he? They hadn't even spent any time together socially. All he knew was what Randall was like to work with, not how he behaved with friends, or whether he had any funny ideas about politics. Hell, what if he hated art? What if he hated stubble?

Jay's words still played on his mind. Would it be a good idea to find someone? Was it even possible for Ellis to have a relationship?

He didn't know a thing about Randall other than what he did for a living. Was the dog trainer older than Ellis? Younger? Did he have family in London? His accent placed him somewhere around the East End, so surely he had family somewhere. How exactly would Ellis explain that he couldn't attend weddings, funerals, dinners, or any other events that took place before sunset?

It was a waste of time wallowing in his teen-like romanticising of his feelings for Randall. If they somehow overcame the short-term problems, and if by some miracle Randall accepted what he was, there was the lingering problem of Ellis' supposed longevity. Barring another Blitz, which according to Jonas was responsible for wiping out vampires far older than the Tower of London, Ellis should live for hundreds or thousands of years. How could he possibly face losing someone and then living on without them for that length of time?

Perhaps vampires gave up on relationships with mortals altogether and only dated each other. Doing that dwindled Ellis' odds of finding anyone: it was difficult enough to find love as a gay man while still alive. He'd dated, he'd had relationships come and go, but he hadn't ever found someone to spend forever with.

God, he realised, he hadn't been on a date in two years. He'd only been a vampire half that time.

How could he find London's two or three other gay vampires without freedom of movement, anyway? Crossing through the territories of others could lead to his destruction, so he was mostly confined to his own turf, wandering Mayfair and straying into the north of Westminster to walk Tiberius. Only the Council of Elders, their personal Vassals, and the Constabulary were allowed to cross territorial boundaries with impunity; everyone else had the right to do so once a year when it was time for the annual census. The Council didn't travel to do the census; every vampire in London had to travel to them, and failure to show was as good as relinquishing your claim to your territory. It all sounded ridiculously ritualised, but it worked well at keeping the population down and preventing skirmishes on the street.

Even if he found them, he probably wouldn't get on with them. It was better to stick to Mayfair. He'd made it clear with Jonas' death that he was more than capable of defending himself, and since he didn't lay claim to Jonas' own turf, whatever squabble ensued over it stayed well away from him.

By Thursday, Ellis was in a proper funk. They walked down to Green Park together and repeated the training Tiberius already had. It was tedious in one regard; if Ellis had wanted to spend his time doing the same action again and again he would've got some data-entry job or something. On the other hand he enjoyed spending time with Tiberius, and it gave him plenty of time to dream up random situations in which a relationship with Randall might work out.

It was all fantasy, of course. Maybe there was something out there that could restore Ellis to humanity, or Randall was secretly a vampire who could fake a heartbeat and warmth and everything else it took to appear so inviting. There would be wild nights of sex, and days laid wrapped around each other's bodies while the world was locked out of their little haven.

In one of Jonas' more poetic moments he had drawled on about the vampire as a solitary figure; a hunter who was forever trapped outside the mortal world, yet doomed to feed on it. He had been very keen on the doomed part, as though he were labouring under some eternal curse meted out by gods thousands of years ago, when man still hid in caves and smashed rocks together to make fire. It was more romantic, Ellis supposed, than it simply being a disease or some sort of magic. Jonas was certainly the type of fella who liked to feel chosen, and what could garner more sympathy than a terrible curse which doomed all souls it touched?

He hated thinking about Jonas. He much preferred to consider Randall.

It kept coming back to Randall, didn't it? Whenever he woke up, he idly considered what Randall might be up to that time of day. A shower was an excuse to think of sharing it with a warm body. His walk with Tiberius reminded him that he would soon return to the park with Randall at his side, his heart picking up with joy and arousal whenever Ellis dropped a double entendre in his lap.

And now here they were, walking back and forth, putting Tiberius through his paces, and still all Ellis could do was daydream about a man whose face he could never see.

"Can I ask you something?" he blurted. It was as though his subconscious had stolen control of his mouth just long enough to force the words out, and Ellis trapped his lip between his teeth. It was like shutting the gate after the horse had bolted.

"Yeah, of course."

God, he was so sweet. He didn't hesitate at all, did he? Whatever Ellis wanted, Randall was ready to provide.

Ellis cleared his throat. "What do you look like?"

And there it was: the little leap in Randall's heart rate, his minute intake of breath. Each little sound was part of an orchestra, softly playing Randall's emotions out for Ellis to hear.

"Well, um. I'm..." Randall was *shy*. His voice caught and lowered as though finding some way of describing himself to another would make him think about his appearance too closely. "I'm five foot eight.

I dunno. I kept waiting for a growth spurt and it never came." His laugh was weak. "Uh, anyway. I keep myself in shape, work out a bit, but I'm not like some muscled-up beefcake, you know. I'm black, and my eyes are, like, sort of dark brown. I don't do anything mental with my hair, uh. It's just cut close. It goes a bit afro if I don't."

Ellis smiled a little and asked Tiberius to sit, then he faced Randall. "Mind if I look?"

"Look?" Randall's pulse spiked higher.

Ellis chuckled. "Well it sounds better than 'mind if I put my hands all over your face?'"

"Oh!" Randall's voice wavered, and a twinge of excitement made his exclamation lilt upward as it ended. "Yeah, of course. Um, I mean. Yeah, go for it."

He wants this, Ellis thought. *He wants me to touch him.*

God, was this all about to become an awful mistake? Randall liked him every bit as much as he liked Randall, it seemed. That could only bring problems. It couldn't last even if they did have feelings for each other. Hell, it probably couldn't even get off the starting block.

Randall's breathing was quick as he waited.

Ellis gently lowered Tiberius' harness and told the dog to stay, then he raised his hands to Randall's chest and placed his fingertips lightly over his heart. The vibration of it could be felt through his ribs and the hard muscle that covered them. It transferred through the soft cotton of Randall's t-shirt along with the warmth from his blood, and Ellis' body leaned toward him, drawn in by a magnetism he didn't want to understand.

He forced his hands upward. He wanted to cling to Randall's body, to learn every line of it, but not here. Not in the middle of the park. And certainly not without asking first. His palms joined in the exploration mission as he found his way over the collar of Randall's t-shirt and straight to the bumps of exposed collarbone and softness of his throat.

Randall's breath came in hurried gasps. His muscles quivered with the effort of staying still.

Ellis drew his fingers up the sides of Randall's neck. His touch was unhurried, a soft tease to feed Randall's anticipation. Ellis knew he was being a bugger. He could've asked Randall to guide him straight to his face, but then where would the fun be?

It was an excuse to touch him, and he was damn well going to take the opportunity.

His hands passed over Randall's jaw. He stroked over his ears and then followed the strong jawline down to the slight cleft in his chin. Randall's skin was taut over the muscles and bones, and Ellis spread his fingers to feel for the slight hollows in his cheeks, the intensity of his cheekbones. His thumbs felt along those clearly-defined ridges and then across to his straight, strong nose before they found their goal.

Randall's lips.

They parted a little at Ellis' touch, pouring hot breath over his skin. His lips were soft and full, with a touch of moisture toward the centre and a delicate collection of ridges formed from their relaxation. Ellis slipped one thumb just a little further over Randall's lower lip until he crossed the border between moist and wet. With slow and deliberate care he drew his dampened thumb back across Randall's lower lip.

The faintest of sounds, imperceptible to anyone else, broke free from Randall's throat. A tiny strangled whimper, heavy with desire.

Holy fuck, he was gorgeous.

He heard Randall's clothing shift, felt the body under his hands move, and Randall's warmth drew around him until it touched his face in return. His hands cupped Ellis' cheeks as Ellis' held Randall's. His fingers splayed into Ellis' hair and his soft palms came to rest over his cheeks. Randall's heart raced along ten to the dozen.

There was nowhere else to go from here. Ellis couldn't have pulled away if he'd wanted to. Randall's lips were within his reach, and he had an open invitation to meet them with his own.

Only a fucking idiot turned that down.

Ellis pressed his chest to Randall's and lowered his head. He knew where Randall's mouth was. It waited for him, hungry but restrained, while Randall's breath heated the air between them. He breathed in, accepting the heat into his own lungs.

Then his lips met Randall's.

God, there was more to it than that, though. Randall's mouth invited him, each breath pushing warmth and need into Ellis' as he parted his lips and pressed. He felt the hard length in Randall's jeans as it clamoured for attention against his thigh, and the firm buttons of his nipples as they strove to reach him through both their shirts. Randall tasted weakly of tea and salt. His lips tightened against Ellis' as they responded to their presence. Randall's nose bumped against Ellis' cheek, and Ellis slid his tongue forward to caress the delicate skin beyond Randall's outer lips.

Randall's whimper returned, stronger. Longer. Louder. His fingers delved deeper into Ellis' hair, his palms shifted to cup his ears.

Ellis' body thrummed in tune with Randall's pulse. He tipped his head further and butted his tongue against Randall's teeth, and Randall's mouth opened for him.

It didn't matter where they were anymore. He wanted Randall, now.

Ellis needed him.

God, he *needed* him.

TWELVE

RANDALL'S INSIDES felt like a churning mass; hard need bubbled through the parts of him that melted and sought to collapse. Ellis' mouth had claimed him and he was helpless in its grasp.

They were kissing. Holy shit they were kissing.

This was totally unprofessional.

Ellis' tongue took control of his mouth, and from there his entire body. His fingers were cool against Randall's cheeks. His kiss was like he'd come to the kiss straight after a cold drink, and his hair was so silky and fine between Randall's fingers. His hands began to move back down Randall's neck-

He gasped for air and exhaled in a long moan. Ellis' hands roamed over his chest, where they scraped and squeezed, pinched and caressed. His touch was deft and certain as it explored down over his ribs and to his hips.

He was supposed to find out whether Ellis was a vampire. His job, his orders... Not *this*. Not falling under the taller man's spell. Not feeling the swell of arousal as it coursed through his blood and pushed him against Ellis' lithe, lean frame.

Ellis' fingers clenched Randall's hips and pulled them against his thigh. There was no way Ellis couldn't feel Randall's hard-on now, surely. Christ, he *had* to know.

Randall's chest heaved. The moon was too near full. His body was fuelled by animal instinct. The wolf was close to the surface, and Briar wasn't here to help Randall claw himself back on top of it.

One of Ellis' hands left Randall's hip and sought his groin. His palm cupped around the bulge in Randall's jeans, first to slip between his legs, and then to rub slowly up the length of it with every ounce of care he had taken over Randall's face.

Randall bucked against Ellis' hand and released a plaintive cry against his tongue.

Ellis withdrew his hand. Worse, he lifted his head back and broke the kiss. Randall tried desperately to read his expression, but his glasses masked too much.

"I'm sorry," Ellis whispered. "I... went too far."

Randall tried to say no, to insist that Ellis hadn't gone anywhere near far enough. All that came out was another choked-off plea without words to make sense of it.

Ellis sucked his own lip in a way Randall found indescribably sexy, but he leaned back a little further, and Randall's hands fell from his hair to land helpless against Ellis' chest. "I understand," Ellis added, voice on a more even keel, "if you no longer wish to work with me. I can ask Jay to call on another trainer. That was completely out of order. I don't-" Ellis paused to take a breath. "I don't think you have any idea how beautiful you are."

Randall groaned and dragged his hands away from Ellis' body. They hung at his sides instead, limp and useless while he fought the voice inside him that told him to return them back where they'd just come from.

The kiss had been enough to inflame his heart and turn his thoughts to mush. Ellis was gorgeous, and confident, and intelligent and perfect. His touch sent fizz through his veins. It brought him to life like he'd lived a dream up until that very moment and had only now woken from it.

But Randall had orders.

Ellis' flesh was cool to the touch, but not cold. Not like he might think a vampire's would be. What if he had poor circulation, or some other medical reason for simply being a bit chilly? What if that jacket was just thin, and the night air had got through it? Ellis dressed nicely but his clothes didn't exactly look warm.

And what if he *was* a vampire? What if he wasn't at all interested in Randall - not romantically, at least. What if this was how he hunted? It would make sense for a blind creature with a lair to distract and arouse his prey before luring him into the trap. Was this how a vampire fed, or whatever it was they did? Did they seduce the living and then drink their blood once they were too blinded themselves to understand what had happened? Like a fly in a web, would Randall struggle to be free even as the last of his life was sucked from him?

If it was a trap, Randall had a significant advantage. Human prey might be unable to escape, but Randall could call on other shapes, and if a wolf's body wasn't enough for him to slip free then taking on the halfway form should do it.

Half way. It was a misleading term, but nobody wanted to use the real word, the one that sat on the tip of their tongues when they spoke of it.

Monster.

Ten feet tall. Close to four hundred pounds of muscle and fang, with claws the length of a man's finger. There was nothing "half" about the horrific shape a wolf shifter could call on when he needed to fight for his life.

If Ellis did try to feed from him, that would be the proof Randall needed, right? And if Ellis wasn't a vampire Randall would be a bloody idiot to pass up on this chance.

"No." Randall found his voice at last. "You didn't take it too far."

It was nowhere near far enough.

Ellis' features broke into a broad, relieved smile. "Well, then maybe we should do this properly. Let me take you to dinner tomorrow. Say, eight o'clock?"

Randall's head spun. "Eight."

"Aye. Meet me at my office?" Ellis grinned.

There was a flight of butterflies competing to escape Randall's stomach. Tomorrow evening. A dinner date. With Ellis.

He nodded hard. "Yes!"

THE WAIT WAS LESS than twenty-four hours, and it was a torment unlike anything Randall had endured before. He slept badly and drifted through Friday utterly unable to concentrate. He checked the time so often that sometimes only a minute had passed. He went to Oxford Street and bought himself a new shirt.

When he arrived at the gallery he was half an hour early, so he hid in Costa nursing a mug of tea because it was better than pacing outside the gallery trying to summon the courage to walk through the doors. With five minutes to go he hurried out and down the Mews to the O'Neill Gallery so that he could walk in the door bang on time.

Ellis awaited him, fingers at his wristwatch. He wore dark trousers with a matching jacket, and a deep orange shirt. Tiberius' tail swished happily when he saw Randall.

Ellis' grin was infectious, and Randall let it lure him into releasing his own.

"Shall we?" Ellis offered his arm.

Randall glanced up the stairs and caught Jay beaming like a bridesmaid. He laughed and took Ellis' arm. "Sure. Where to?"

Ellis urged Tiberius on, and Randall opened the door, then followed after Ellis.

"The Coach and Horses. Just off Bruton Lane."

"I've no idea where that is. Do we need a taxi?"

Ellis laughed gently. "No, it's all right. I know the way."

It was only a ten minute dawdle away, and it turned out to be a beautiful traditional old pub with black lacquer doors and a welcoming interior. Randall was surprised to find something so homely in the heart of Mayfair, but relieved as hell too; his new shirt was nice, but he didn't think he'd get away with trying to wear it in some of the district's posher places.

A table had been booked, and they were led to it by a cheerful waiter who thought Tiberius was adorable but didn't seem too sure what to do about the dog. He looked even less certain how to handle a blind customer, but Ellis revealed he'd already had Jay read him the menu from their website and had picked out what he wanted. On the downside, this meant Randall felt the urge to pick quickly from an unfamiliar menu, despite Ellis' insistence that there was no rush.

"Now then," Ellis murmured once their meals were ordered. "You should tell me about yourself."

Randall laughed a little. "Er. Well, there's not really that much to tell."

"Rubbish. Don't dare pretend you're boring. Spill the beans, Randall."

He glanced to the table, but the old varnished wood wasn't any help. "Well, er. I'm twenty-eight. Born and raised in Spitalfields. I've got an older brother." He reached for his ale when it arrived and sipped warily, but it was as real as the menu had claimed, free from the tang and bitterness of chemicals. "Our dad left when I was ten. Anyway." Randall shrugged as he tried to work out how to skip the part about finding out he was a werewolf. "I always liked dogs. I dunno. We had one when we were little and he never betrayed us, you know?"

"I understand." Ellis spoke softly.

"Yeah. So for ages I wanted to be a vet, but I was rubbish at school and never got the GCSEs for it."

Ellis was silent, paying attention, but with a speculative look on his features that suggested he didn't quite buy the story.

"Fine." Randall sighed. "I realised that vets have to put healthy animals down. I couldn't do it. I went into animal psychology instead. After that I moved to Stepney and set up my business."

Ellis smiled faintly. "There's no shame in *not* being a killer." He idly checked the position of cutlery and cruet on the table. "I've got two brothers, both older. Dad's a solicitor, and they were all about following in his footsteps. I was dead keen on being an artist, but I never really had the talent for it, so I ponced some cash off dad and came down south to start a gallery. First off all I could afford was this little room over another place, but over time it's grown and now we're in Mayfair."

"Down south?" Randall paused as dinner arrived, then added "Where're you from originally?"

"York."

"I would've thought York would be a great place for a gallery business."

Ellis chuckled. "It would be, except my obnoxious family's there." His slender shoulders shrugged in a slow, idle gesture. "I'd need to find a Russian oligarch who wants a dedicated art source to pay Dad back. There's this idea that galleries are rolling in money, but when you only really shift a handful of pieces a month it's barely enough to cover the rent, rates and insurance, let alone our wages."

"Really?" Randall blinked. "'Cause I've seen some of your prices-"

Ellis laughed now. "I know. And our commission's fifty percent. It's that good old Catch-22. If you want to attract the international money you have got to locate in Mayfair, but Mayfair costs so much that galleries are going out of business at a terrifying rate."

"You're okay, though?"

Ellis bit his lip. "We're okay. But we're a young gallery. You have to be at this game for decades or, better yet, generations."

"There go all my dreams of meeting a rich gallery owner and living a life of luxury." Randall laughed, and Ellis snorted.

Watching Ellis eat was an intriguing pleasure. The art dealer made short work of using his knife and fork as probes to figure out the location of the food on his plate, then cut it into neat, bite-sized pieces, occasionally checking the new positioning of all his items. It happened with practised ease as they spoke, and Ellis hardly seemed to pay any attention to the activity.

"Can I ask something?" Randall paused eating his own meal and chewed the inside of his cheek.

"Aye."

"No, I mean it's pretty personal. And, I dunno. Maybe it's rude."

Ellis' lips twitched with amusement. "Then I insist. Ask away."

"What's it like running a business, especially an art business, with a visual impairment?"

"Fair question. It's got its challenges. I've had to learn to trust Jay's judgement on pieces we get sent for consideration, but he has excellent taste." He laughed easily, which put Randall slightly more at ease. "After all, he married Han. Other than that there are workarounds. The stuff on offer to help out is pretty bloody awesome. There's a company that makes canes with sensors in them like the things they put in car bumpers. Distance sensors. Then there's other stuff in them that can tell up and down, north and south. I suppose they nicked the compass stuff out of a phone for it. But then what it does is it gives you all this information through different vibrations in the handle. It's genius."

Randall looked up in surprise. "That's pretty sweet! Have you got one?"

Ellis chuckled and shook his head. "Nah. I've got Tiberius. Don't need both, and he's better company than a stick. Here," he added, and dipped one hand into his jacket pocket. He withdrew something about the size of a book and offered it to Randall.

Randall took it. It was a plastic case, so he popped it open and found a miniature version of the braille display from Ellis' office.

"What's this?" he asked, running his fingers over the rounded pins. It felt like a neat arrangement of tiny ball bearings.

"It's a Bluetooth braille display." Ellis beamed. "Connects to my phone so I can send and receive emails, texts, all that stuff."

"Wow." Randall closed the case and handed it back, pressing the case against Ellis' hand until Ellis took it from him and tucked it away.

"Yeah. None of it's cheap, but I don't have to pay the VAT, so there's an extra few bob for dog food." Ellis' grin turned crooked. "My go."

"Your go at what?"

"A personal question." Ellis found his knife and fork again, then said "What's it like being black *and* gay in London?"

"That's pretty bloody personal, yeah," Randall agreed. "Um. Well. I mean, are you asking about racism, or fetishisation, or what?"

"Yep." Ellis ate and feigned innocence.

"Bloody hell." Randall put down his fork and reached for his ale. He took a couple of mouthfuls, then said, "It's kind of... I mean... I suppose it's like how you probably get treated. Everyone likes to go around patting themselves on the back and saying how politically correct they are, then they'll treat you like you're an idiot, or shout hate at something they take a dislike to. Even my mum'll insist she's never encountered racism, that London's not like that. It's like we all pretend it's not an issue, like if we all just say there's no racism here it'll cease to exist. Click your heels together three times." He swallowed again. "And, you know, it seems to work for most people, but I've had clients walk away when they find out I'm black, like a black guy can't possibly know anything about dogs. They never say it, they just find some excuse to cancel." He shrugs. "I dunno. That's probably for the best anyway. If they can't cope with my skin they'll ignore everything I tell 'em anyway. It'd be a self-fulfilling prophecy. Their dog wouldn't improve 'cause they refuse to stick to the programme, then it's all my fault for being terrible and they should have known better."

Ellis listened and nodded. He didn't interrupt, didn't try to assure Randall that racism was some long-dead boogeyman.

"Then you hit the gay scene and it gets a hundred times worse. Guys want this and that, they don't want something or other. They act like there's a menu to choose from, like everyone else on the scene's just an item and they're all customers. I get hit on like I'm some kind of penis god, and you know damn well that's all they're after, 'cause conversation quickly turns to 'is it true what they say about black guys?'"

Ellis' lips tugged playfully and he leaned forward. "You will be pleased to hear, then, that I don't particularly care how big your cock is."

Randall nearly drowned on his ale. He thumped the glass down against the table as the coughing burned his throat, and he had to grab his napkin to mop up the mess. His pulse throbbed in his ears. "Crap," he wheezed.

Ellis' smirk became a filthy grin. "It doesn't matter, because I like to be the one doing the fucking."

Randall gripped his napkin and stared at Ellis.

Had the temperature increased five degrees in here?

Ellis licked his lips and reached for his wallet, then used a card-sized piece of plastic to check the edges of the notes he pulled out.

He dropped £50 on the table, then said "Shall we go?"

Their meals were mostly done. Randall had no interest in finishing his, and it looked like Ellis couldn't care less about his own plate anymore either.

"Yeah. God, yeah."

He tugged his shirt free so that the hem hung over his bulge.

Might as well go with *some* dignity.

THIRTEEN

ELLIS' flat was in a beautiful old building that must once have been a townhouse of some sort. Randall didn't care.

Fuck, he was letting Ellis drag him off home for sex like some kind of caveman. There were only two ways this could go, and one of them led to carnage.

The flat was dark inside. Curtains were closed, and the only light came from LEDs on whatever electronics were scattered around. It wasn't enough to see by, not with his human eyes.

He made vague note of a wealth of locks on the door of Ellis' flat, but Ellis didn't spend any time locking them. It felt less like a trap that way.

Maybe it was supposed to.

Ellis only released him to take Tiberius' harness off. Randall heard the rip of Velcro in the dark, and the plastic sound of something placed on a hard surface. He didn't dare move in case the werespider theory turned out to be true.

He tried not to laugh at the absurdity of it all.

"You all right?" Ellis breathed, suddenly close again.

Randall gulped. "Yeah. It's just dark. I can't really see much."

"It's fine. Let me show you."

Ellis' fingers slid down Randall's arms and then curled around his hands, and Randall clutched them like a lifeline.

"Follow me." Ellis tugged as he spoke.

Randall let Ellis lead him through the alien landscape and forced himself to take slow breaths. He was behaving like a child. Ellis' whole world was this dark, and Randall was getting worked up over a single flat.

Admittedly it could be a flat of death. But that didn't count; Randall's other shapes could see in here, and if he needed to use them he'd be fine.

Ellis turned him and pushed him back. His calves nudged against something soft, so Randall did as he was told and sat.

It was a bed.

Randall laughed, suddenly nervous. "Bloody hell. You don't hang about, do you?"

Ellis' chuckle came closer. His knees straddled Randall's lap, and he leaned against the shorter man until Randall took the hint and lay back on the mattress. "Don't worry. I won't bite."

"Oh?" It came out more strangled than Randall had aimed for.

"Nibble, maybe. Suck, absolutely. Lick, you bet I will. Biting's for people who lose control."

Randall groaned. He was hard again, just like that. His groin pulsed with lust over a handful of words scattered like confetti against his lips. He drew breath, but Ellis kissed him and stole it away again.

He was already lost, and Ellis hadn't even begun.

Soft stubble brushed against his jaw once Ellis broke from the kiss. Cool lips teased Randall's ear, followed by a trail of tongue that followed the curve of his earlobe. Randall moaned and shivered when Ellis' tongue continued up the outer edge of his ear, and when Ellis' lips found their way back to his own he pressed eagerly into the kiss. His hands found Ellis' thighs and squeezed them, and Ellis' groin pressed into his own.

Ellis was hard as a rock. Their clothed lengths crushed together, millimetres of fabric the only thing between them, and Ellis' deft fingers found the top button of Randall's shirt while his lips trapped Randall's and sucked one, then the other. Button after button squeezed through each buttonhole, and every one loosened Randall's shirt more. Soft fingers eased under the fabric and pushed it aside until Ellis' hands were flush against Randall's skin.

Ellis released his mouth and sat up. His hands wandered slowly as they explored Randall's chest. His fingers dipped around Randall's sides and fanned out as he pulled back toward his breastbone. His palms grazed over Randall's hard nipples, which elicited another sharp gasp. Randall's chest lifted, his back arched, and his cock throbbed almost painfully.

"Ellis," he whimpered.

"I'll get to it," Ellis whispered into the darkness.

"Okay," was all Randall could come out with.

Ellis' hands traced over Randall's stomach, and then the man's lips drifted across his collarbone, and Randall threw his head back with a guttural plea. Ellis didn't hurry. There was no rush to his actions. His lips would create an airtight seal so that he could suck softly on small patches of Randall's skin, and then his cool, wet tongue lapped over the spot as he made his way down Randall's chest to follow his own hands.

Randall lay like a pinned butterfly, his shoes barely able to reach the floor. Ellis *saw* him. He touched Randall with all the care and attention that he had lavished on the trainer's face last night, and through his hands he was *looking* at Randall's body, something Randall was unable to do in return. He felt helpless and dominated at the same time, but not the kind of dominance the pack threw around like playground bullies. This was different.

Ellis wasn't demanding anything of him, yet there was no doubt who was in control. Randall's obedience, his submission, it wasn't something bitten and beaten out of him; it was something he gave willingly.

Was he okay with that? Was it all right to have some part of himself that wanted to belong to Ellis?

Ellis' body twisted as his hands snaked between them still. They dipped to Randall's fly and unfastened the button. The zip rasped and eased the pressure against Randall's cock.

And then Ellis' long, slender fingers pushed beneath the waist of Randall's briefs and curled around his shaft.

What Ellis did next definitely didn't involve his teeth.

He writhed down Randall's body and enveloped Randall's cock in his brisk mouth while his hand remained firm around the root of it. He suckled and lapped as his head bobbed along the length, and all

Randall could do was fumble blindly for Ellis' hair and grip the soft strands as he begged and keened for more.

Randall didn't stand a chance.

By the time Ellis wriggled back up his body, Randall was close. When he heard another zip and felt Ellis' cock slide against his own, he was teetering on the edge. And when Ellis' hand clamped around them both and stroked their lengths together, he cried out a warning.

"Do it," Ellis whispered, his voice hoarse, almost savage.

Randall bucked. His muscles clenched until only his shoulders and arse were in contact with the bed. The force of his orgasm tore him apart, and the sound that came from him wasn't a cry.

It was a howl.

He shuddered against the sheets, body convulsing as the last of it rippled through him. Ellis released him before sensitivity could transform the contact from pleasure to agony, and while Randall's body was still refusing to regain any semblance of control he heard Ellis' soft, short grunt, and felt his oddly chill juices mingle with his own on his stomach.

"Fuck," Ellis groaned. His head sank to the crook of Randall's neck and buried itself there, and Randall finally realised Ellis wasn't wearing his sunglasses anymore.

Randall agreed with a mumbled moan and lay in the silence until he had the strength to move his arms and wrap them around Ellis' still-clothed waist. "Speaking of fucking," he eventually said, a grin tugging at his lips, "where's mine?"

Ellis laughed weakly. "What? Are you in some kind of hurry?"

"Well, no, but-" Randall tilted so that he could kiss Ellis' jaw, then grinned again at the sensation of stubble against his lips. "Pretty sure you were the one who brought it up."

"Stop by my office tomorrow, I'll see what we can do." Ellis felt his way to the sheets either side of Randall's shoulders, and slowly prised himself upward. "Shower?"

"Shower," Randall agreed.

THE BATHROOM WAS BRIGHTLY LIT. Light had flooded it when

Ellis switched the extractor fan on, only to apologise profusely when he'd heard Randall's swearing.

Randall had peeled his shirt off fully, along with the rest of his clothes, and then watched with an odd sense of voyeurism as Ellis did the same. The taller man's body was fit without being musclebound, and as pale as Randall might expect of a Yorkshireman who spent most of his time indoors and worked well into the evenings.

There was an old-looking white bathtub with ornate feet. It sat on black and white chequered tile flooring, beside a toilet and bidet pair, and an equally old-looking white sink. The end of the bathroom was separated by a sheet of glass for a walk-in shower that had no door, and a wall-to-ceiling heated towel rack lined the space alongside the door. Walls were lined with smooth white handrails. It was as neat and flawless as the gallery, and Randall assumed that the darkened apartment was the same.

They showered together. The enclosure was easily large enough to accommodate them both, and as Randall faced Ellis under the hot water and his eyes had grown accustomed to the light, he saw Ellis' eyes.

They were like ice. Blue, but only barely, and with an odd refraction that Randall could have sworn rendered them faintly luminous. That had to be a trick of the light. It was just a lack of pigment in the iris, nothing... odd.

Nothing supernatural.

Right?

Randall shivered as Ellis ran soap and skin across his body. "Ellis."

"What's up?"

"You, uh." He cleared his throat. "Your flat's dark. I mean, pitch black."

Ellis' lips curled apologetically. "Sorry. I didn't think about that. I'll have to show you where the light switches are."

"Don't you ever open the curtains?"

Ellis' unfocused eyes flit toward Randall's face, and then down. "Nah. What's the point?"

"I just thought, well. You can still see a bit when it's light, yeah?"

"Mm." Ellis shrugged, and cupped his hands against Randall's chest to sweep water and suds away. "Going blind once was bad enough. I don't like doing it on a daily basis, so I just keep them shut, keep the lights off."

Randall searched Ellis' gaze, but it didn't meet him.

"You can see now, right?" Randall said quietly.

Ellis' chest rose as he took a breath, then he lifted his head and looked to Randall. "To some degree of the word 'see'," he answered, a touch of bitterness to his voice, "yes."

Randall bit his lip, then leaned in closer. "What about now?"

He watched as Ellis' eyes flicked back and forth, saw his eyebrows come down in concentration and his eyes narrow in sympathy with them. Ellis was forced to look at each little piece of Randall's face, he realised, and assemble a picture from whatever snapshots he managed to glean. More than that, though, it took effort.

"Well," Ellis murmured at last, his features relaxing again. "That's confirmed."

"What is?"

"You're beautiful."

Randall broke into a sheepish laugh and looked away. "Says you."

"Oh I know beauty, Randall, believe me." Ellis' lips tugged again, and he turned the water off, then reached for a handrail and stepped out of the shower. He used the rail as a guide until he reached the towel rack, then wrapped one around himself and offered another toward Randall.

Randall shook himself off and followed, taking the towel with thanks and stealing a look at Ellis' bum while they dried off in companionable silence.

True to his word, Ellis hadn't bitten him.

Was that it, then? Was that the test? If Ellis were some kind of predator, Randall wasn't his prey. Well, not in any way Randall didn't enjoy.

He felt a dirty grin emerge and didn't bother to try and stop it.

God, this was perfect! Ellis wasn't a vampire, so Randall didn't have to kill him, and Briar would want to know as soon as possible. If Randall left soon he could get home, grab some sleep, then be at the garage first thing in the morning to pass on the news.

And then Randall could see Ellis tomorrow night and they could fuck like bunnies.

He grabbed his clothes and pulled them on, but Ellis didn't do the same, and it suddenly occurred to Randall that Ellis might have expected him to stay.

"Er." He drew his sleeves up his arms and straightened his collar, but didn't fasten his buttons just yet. "So you were serious, right? I'll come get you from your office tomorrow?"

"I'm serious." Ellis reached for him.

Randall lifted his hand and took Ellis'. His skin was warm now, after the shower. Randall would have to get him a thicker coat for Christmas or something. "Eight?"

"Eight," Ellis agreed. He stepped closer and leaned in for a kiss.

Randall tipped his head back to welcome it.

Their skin touched, and Randall's breath hitched.

"I'll be there," he promised.

FOURTEEN

WHATEVER JAY SAID, Ellis wasn't listening. He fiddled with his keyboard, head full of last night, and couldn't give a shit if Jay was halfway through handing in his notice.

Was it eight o'clock yet? Would Randall show? He'd sounded certain last night, but what if today he'd changed his mind?

There'd been no texts, no messages. And while Ellis was glad Randall hadn't tried to stay the night, a day later it felt weird.

Had it been a one-night stand?

No. No, not after a date. You didn't bother with a date if you just wanted a quick shag.

Mind you, Ellis hadn't shared a bed with anyone for ages, and certainly not since he'd been turned.

Had he done it wrong?

Had Randall wanted him to go further?

He tapped his fingernails against his desk, then stopped; the *rat-tat-tat* they made grated on his thoughts.

"-away with the fairies, aren't you?"

Ellis gave a non-committal grunt. "Sorry. Miles away."

"Uh huh. Where?"

Ellis tapped the desk again, then admitted "Randall and I had a date last night."

"Oh my god!" Jay squealed. "How did it go? Where'd you go? Tell me everything!"

"Went to a pub, left halfway through, took him back to mine for things you're far too young to hear about."

"You dirty bastards!" Jay laughed. "No wonder you're off in cloud cuckoo land!"

"Maybe." Ellis ran his fingers along the edge of his keyboard, then pulled out the drawer and tucked the reader away in it. "We had deliveries today?"

"Just a couple." Jay moved away to goods in to fetch one, and Ellis heard the crinkle of paper. "You know, when I met Han I fancied the pants off him right away, but what could I do? It was a job interview. I couldn't start flirting then and there."

He heard the rustle of paper against his desk, and smiled dryly. Sometimes canvasses would arrive in cardboard packaging, sometimes with packing chips or polystyrene corners. Other times they'd arrive wrapped in parcel paper and bubble wrap, which was a brave as hell move usually made by artists who didn't understand how careless couriers could be. Ellis reached for it and found parcel paper.

"Anyway," Jay continued, "I got the job, obviously, and he must've known, 'cause he started making appointments I *had* to be there for, you know?" He chuckled. "Errands I needed to run, stuff that kept me after hours, and I was like 'you know if you want me all to yourself you don't have to schedule it, you just need to ask, right?'"

Ellis smiled to himself. "You think this is what I did with Randall?"

"Oh come on. Isn't it?"

Ellis felt around the paper until he found the tape, then he worked at it with care, picking at it until he had enough of a grip to tear it free. "You're a sod," he chuckled. "When are you two off to Paris?"

"About seven in the morning."

"City airport?"

"Eurostar. Caviar at St. Pancras for breakfast!" Jay laughed easily.

Ellis crinkled his nose and tugged the paper free. There wasn't any bubblewrap beneath it, just the canvas, and he spread his fingers around the edge with care to check whether it was dry. "Caviar," he muttered. "You two are horrible."

"Just because *you* can't eat-"

"My taste buds still work, thanks." Ellis didn't want to go into the horrid things he had to do to empty his stomach if he'd eaten, lest it do so of its own accord at sunrise. "What am I looking at?"

"Er. Let me find the consignment note." Jay walked away again. "Anyway, your temp is called Elaine, and she'll be here to open up tomorrow at noon."

"She's got the keys?" Ellis slid his hands across the canvas. It felt like acrylic paint, but without the smoothness of varnish.

"She's got my keys. I've walked her through as much as she'll need for the next few days, then sent her off home at five. She's nice. I like her."

Ellis nodded absently and focused on the paint beneath his touch.

Hatred. Vile, rolling loathing. So little light, so many sketches.

Sketches of Ellis.

A man he didn't recognise worked in a poorly-lit flat with a canvas that he had purchased ready-made, ready-stretched. He primed it with a wash of black, then went straight at it with no underpainting. He referred now and then to the sketches of Ellis which lined the canvas.

He was a young man, maybe Jay's age - mid-twenties. He had short brown hair and deep blue eyes, and a strong nose with thin lips. He worked feverishly as time skidded forward, daubing pale skin onto the canvas as though he were driving a knife home. The painting grew quickly; the artist was skilled, though his style was hurried.

Brutal.

Sometimes Ellis thought he caught a glimpse of someone else in the darkness, watching the painting unfold. Other times the artist worked alone. He never spoke.

There was something wrong with the figure he painted. Face twisted into a frozen scream, his centre was rotting until there was nothing but a hole where his heart should be.

No, not rotting.

Time flickered, and a spatter of paint appeared.

Ash. He was turning to ash.

A second figure became visible on the canvas. Brown hair. The artist himself, maybe; he painted this figure with pain and loss rather than loathing.

The last thing to be painted was the shaft of silver which penetrated the hole where Ellis' heart should have been.

The weapon he intended to kill Ellis with.

"Ellis! *Ellis!*"

He could hear screaming.

"Oh, god, Ellis!" Jay had grabbed one of his hands and was pulling on it. "Stop! It's okay! Let go!"

Ellis drew breath to scream again. His body shook with terror, and the blackness that replaced his vision didn't help.

Jay changed tactics, and the canvas was dragged away from Ellis' hands by force.

Ellis sobbed as he sagged against the desk.

"Ellis? Jay? What's wrong? You guys okay?"

Jay's heart thudded in panic. Ellis' would have, if it still beat at all.

"Randall?" he managed to whisper.

FIFTEEN

RANDALL STARED at the tableau in the office. Ellis and Jay looked like guilty schoolchildren caught with their hands jammed in the biscuit barrel together, and both of them were pale as ghosts.

He'd thought it would be a good idea to show up early. Ellis had said eight, but it was pretty much a booty call. Who didn't rush to turn up for sex?

Instead of a warm welcome, Randall had arrived to screams and shouting, and rushed up the stairs to find Jay tearing a painting out of Ellis' hands while Ellis screamed his head off.

Now Jay was frozen in terror, and Ellis gripped the edge of his desk.

"I'm fine," Ellis rasped.

"Fine," Jay echoed. Then he sprang into action and shoved the canvas behind himself.

Randall might have found it comical if the pair of them didn't look so afraid.

Ellis dropped his left hand behind the desk, and Randall heard a faint whine from Tiberius as Ellis found and fussed his dog.

"You two are really crap liars," Randall muttered. "What's going on? And don't you dare say 'nothing'."

"Just, uh-" Ellis began.

"Really, *really* bad art," Jay finished, babbling quickly. "Oh you wouldn't believe how bad! And you know what art people are like. We are so prone to histrionics, we'll squeal at anything! I should return this to the artist and tell him it made us lose our dinners-"

"Show me," Randall said.

"You don't want to see it," Ellis said, shifting in his seat like he might stand. He turned towards Randall, his features set in a desperate plea.

"How about I just toss it out?" Jay sidled toward the door. "I'll throw it, sweetie."

Randall grit his teeth and let Jay past, then turned and snatched at the canvas' wooden frame. Jay's struggle was brief, and his hold on the painting wasn't a strong one.

"No-" Jay bit back his cry.

Randall stepped quickly away from him, then turned the canvas and lifted it so that he could look.

"Jay?" Ellis asked.

Jay made a strangled sound. "He... Randall..."

Randall stared at the painting. Two figures, locked in deadly combat, and one of them was unmistakably Ellis.

Well, except the Ellis in the painting had fangs, and seemed to be turning to dust.

It could have been some sort of statement from an angry artist; someone might see the gallery industry as sucking the lifeblood out of the art scene, and picked a random gallery owner to transform into a vampire to make his point. But if that were the case, why in the name of arse did Ellis and Jay look so bloody shamefaced?

"What?" Ellis asked.

"I took the painting," Randall explained. His voice trembled.

Ellis froze.

Jay moved like a marionette and shut the office door, then leaned against it, staring at Randall.

"This looks," Randall said as carefully as he could, "like someone's accusing you of being a vampire."

"It does?" Ellis remained poised to leap from his chair.

"Are you?"

"No! Don't be ridiculous! What kind of question is that?"

Randall closed his mouth and took a deep breath. With Jay this close to him, he stood a chance of smelling something useful, so he concentrated as he inhaled.

Fear.

He opened his eyes again. He hadn't needed to pick out Jay's pheromones to see the man was afraid, but at least his scent was in line with his behaviour.

"Don't lie to me. Please. Not after last night-" Randall broke off and gripped the canvas frame tightly. "Don't." He looked towards Jay, still leaning against the door, and said "You know, don't you?"

Jay's hesitation spoke volumes.

Randall looked to Ellis. "Do you feed on Jay? Is that what this is?"

"No!" Ellis and Jay almost shouted the denial in unison; immediate and vehement, as if the idea repulsed them both.

"You're a vampire." Randall sagged and looked at the painting in his hands. "This is a death threat."

A death threat.

Did it matter? If whomever had painted this didn't kill Ellis, Randall would have to do it himself.

The frame creaked in his hands.

"Randall." Ellis spoke weakly.

Randall tore his gaze from the painting and looked to him. "Why did you scream?"

Ellis' body sank back against his chair, and he sought Tiberius' head again. "I can't tell you," he whispered.

"Jay knows." Randall turned to Jay. "How long have you known?"

"I-" Jay shook his head helplessly.

"For god's sake," Ellis snapped. "All right. Yes. I'm a vampire. Are you happy? Leave Jay alone."

"Of course I'm not bloody happy!" The canvas' frame splintered under his fingers.

Randall had to get control of himself, or Jay would end up smeared in pieces across the office floor. He screwed his eyes shut and tried his damnedest to push his anger down.

"I can see glimpses of the past," Ellis said, resigned. "When I touch something. I get visions of where that thing's been, or what it's been used for. The more powerful the emotions its owner or owners felt when they had it in their possession the more immersive the visions are. I get to feel what the owner felt when they held it."

It sounded absurd.

Thought the werewolf of the vampire.

Randall drew breath and forced himself to open his eyes.

"Objects," Ellis clarified. "Not living things. It doesn't work on animals or people."

Randall licked his lips, then walked to Ellis' desk and put the painting on it. The frame was warped and uneven now. "Do you turn into a flock of bats, too?"

"Is that a blind joke?"

Ellis' jab knocked the wind out of his sails. "No. No, I didn't mean-"

And just like that, Randall was calm again, and Ellis gave a slight nod. "I know. But you sounded like you needed to be derailed. It's okay, Jay," he added.

"What are we going to do?" Jay eased away from the door and hurried to the kettle to focus on making tea. He kept eyeballing Randall, though.

What *was* Randall going to do? He had orders, for crying out loud. Briar wouldn't tolerate fleas, that's what he'd said.

Why did that matter to him so much? Briar's only qualification was that he was bigger and stronger than the rest of the pack, and he had that curious ability which set Alphas apart: he could keep his pack calm during the full moon, keep them from falling to Luna's rage and killing whatever was unfortunate enough to be in the wrong place at the wrong time. Briar turned a ragtag bunch of potential killers into functional people. He allowed them to retain their humanity when the wolf was at its strongest.

Yet here Randall was, on the cusp of the full moon, calm. Upset, yes, but calm.

He stared at Ellis as he lowered himself into the chair that faced the vampire's desk.

Why wasn't Randall leaping across it to tear Ellis' head from his body? How was it that Ellis had been able to puncture Randall's swiftly-bloating fury with a single jab?

Jay sat a mug of tea in front of him, and the sound of ceramic against tabletop made Randall blink. "Thank you," he mumbled.

"Welcome," Jay said, his voice still shaky. He hadn't made a cup for Ellis, Randall noted: just one for Randall and another for himself.

"You aren't going to do anything," Ellis eventually said to Jay.

"I have a train to catch in the morning," Jay fretted, "but that doesn't mean I can't stay until then! Or I could cancel. Han will understand. I can't leave you when there's some crazy person out there threatening to kill you. God, what if I'm in Paris and he succeeds? I can't live with that, Ellis! I can't just pretend everything's okay knowing that I left you and-"

"Han won't understand." Ellis spoke gently, but Jay stopped to listen nonetheless. "He loves you, Jay. He hardly gets to see you. Go to Paris together. It's going to be fine."

Randall gestured to the painting. "If you've seen visions of this picture, what was happening? What did you see that made you scream?"

"I just saw it being painted, but he-" Ellis shook his head and grimaced. "He hates me so much, and I don't know why."

"Well he must know you, 'cause it's not hard to tell it's a painting of you."

"He had sketches. Studies. He'd done studies of me before he got to work on the painting."

Randall grabbed his tea and frowned. "That's a bit-" He hesitated. "That's a bit creepy stalker, isn't it? I mean, it's creepy stalker enough to follow someone around and take pictures, but to bother doing drawings of them?"

Jay sighed and slumped into the chair beside Randall. "They wouldn't be able to take pictures."

"But they probably tried." Randall gripped his mug tight. "Tourists. You heard tourists, right?" He looked to Ellis. "Or you thought it was tourists, but what you heard was a camera."

Ellis nodded, which sent a cascade of hair forward and back. Some got caught in the arms of his glasses, and he brought a hand up to brush those strands free. "Aye."

"What if Tiberius has spent all this time trying to protect you from whoever this is?" Randall glanced to the painting. "What if every time he's led you astray or growled at someone it's been down to this? He knew this bloke wanted to hurt you; he's known all along, and all we did was try to stop him warning you."

"Intelligent disobedience," Ellis breathed. His hand dropped to fuss Tiberius' head again. "God, I... I thought he'd gone off me or something."

"I've watched him with you. He hangs on every word." Randall finally drank some of his tea. "He's loyal to you. I couldn't work out why he was misbehaving, not after this past week's training. He's brilliant."

Ellis smiled down at Tiberius as he ruffled the dog's fur. "He is," he agreed. "Aren't you, boy? Aren't you brilliant!"

"Why couldn't he take pictures?" Randall glanced between the two other men. "Is it the same reason you don't show up in windows or mirrors? Is it a reflection thing?"

Jay blinked.

Ellis lifted his head. "When did you notice that?" he asked carefully.

"A few nights ago."

The room was quiet but for the thud and swish of Tiberius' tail against the floor.

"I don't know," Ellis said at last. "I can't use phones. My voice doesn't get picked up or transmitted by them. I called Jay after I was turned and he didn't hear a thing. When we worked out I didn't have a reflection we tried to map out how far it went so we could find workarounds. I'm not... invisible, I'm not silent. I'm definitely *here* as far as we can tell-" He rapped his knuckles on his desk. "I can use a touch-screen with a stylus, but I can't see the damn things anyway, so I got the portable display. We had to change the security system because the old one had biometrics, so now we've got an older system where anyone with the number can disable the alarm. We've had to refocus the security cameras pretty much onto the stock and nothing else, just in case we ever have to turn footage over to the police for a burglary."

Randall watched him as he spoke. "That's why your route home is so convoluted, right? You're avoiding as much glass as possible."

"There's a lot of CCTV on the main roads, too," Jay grumbled. "It's like a maze."

"And footage of a guide dog walking itself home with its harness up would be proper dodgy," Randall concluded with a sigh. "What're we gonna do?"

"We?" Ellis shook his head. "Randall, everyone in this room could get killed if it gets out that either of you know what I am."

"Yeah, well you're gonna get killed if we sit on our arses and do jack shit."

"I'll cancel," Jay said with finality. "I'll see Han when he comes home."

"Jay, you can't cancel!" Ellis insisted.

"You don't need to," Randall said.

Jay turned his dark eyes on Randall. "What-"

Then Randall said the most foolish thing he could possibly think of to say.

"I'll stay."

Jay blinked. "You what?"

"I won't leave his side until you get back. I will keep an eye out for crazy vampire hunters, and I won't let 'em touch him. Day and night. Nobody lays a finger on him."

Randall's heart was going a mile a minute.

What the *hell* had he just done?

SIXTEEN

ELLIS WANTED TO ARGUE. He wanted to tell Randall to go home and forget everything. If there were some way to rewind the last hour and try it again, that'd be especially useful.

He could hear their hearts pounding with panic. Jay was upset, and wouldn't leave without Randall's assurance, but was that the only reason Randall had given it, or did he have some sort of heroic ideal thrusting its way to the surface? Because that sort of rubbish could get everyone killed.

He was going to die. Again. Oh god, Ellis didn't want to die. The first time had been bad enough.

When the heart was about to stop, the brain knew. There was utter, unflinching certainty about the whole thing. It was a last-ditch effort by every survival instinct lurking deep within the animal psyche, as though screaming an alarm into a dying man's thoughts could somehow make him get up and survive the ordeal. Almost every slow, lingering heart attack was accompanied by terror and a profound sense of impending doom.

Turning someone triggered a heart attack. Not a nice, painless, fast cardiac arrest; the slow, drawn-out hammering horror of a struggling heart. Through it all the victim was helpless, trapped and immobile, subsumed by the orgasmic pleasure of the bite, riding a rollercoaster of rapture and dread all the way to death. It had been the most terrible thing Ellis had ever endured, and there was no way of knowing at the time that he would or even could survive it.

Who the hell wanted Ellis dead? The artist in his vision wasn't remotely familiar to him; not his face, not his style. Nothing about him made sense. What had Ellis done to him?

Or was it vampires the artist had a problem with? How did he know what Ellis was? Had it been so simple as a chance photograph in a public space? Now that cameras were digital and the display was instant, Ellis was in more danger than he could possibly have been even ten years ago. God knew how older vampires coped with the modern world. It was a bloody minefield.

Maybe it was for the best that almost all the elders had died in the Second World War. Poor bastards wouldn't stand a chance nowadays.

"Go home, Jay," he said, "and have a great time in Paris. If you don't go to Le Centre Pompidou I will sack you."

"But-"

"Jay." He idly felt for the corner of his keyboard. It couldn't have moved since he last touched it, but it reassured him to know something was at least where it should be. "If you're in London the whole time you can't stay with me. You have to go home sooner or later. You're not a bodyguard, you're my friend, and I can't let you put yourself in harm's way. Go home. Go to Paris in the morning. Eat caviar then sit on the Eurostar reeking of it. I will text you every day and tell you that I'm fine, I promise, and when you get back we can work out who this fella is and who pissed in his cornflakes, all right?"

He listened as heart rates began to lower. Jay's breathing was a little ragged, but he'd get that under control soon enough.

"Ellis." Jay whined like a child sent to the headmaster's office.

"No. Go home. I'll tell Han you're on your way." He fished the portable display out of his pocket.

Jay huffed. "No need. I'm going. You better take care of him," he added, presumably to Randall, "or I will be super rude about you on Yelp."

"I will," Randall stated.

There was an ounce of doubt in Randall's words, but thankfully Jay didn't pick up on them. He came around the desk to hug Ellis, and whispered "Don't you dare die."

"Wouldn't dare," Ellis murmured.

Jay squeezed his shoulders and stormed off out of the office, and Ellis listened to him clatter down the stairs until he was sure Jay had left the building.

"I've still got questions," Randall muttered.

"Of course you have. But let's go to mine if you're serious about being my hero."

THEY WALKED TOGETHER IN SILENCE, and once they were at the flat Ellis closed the front door, then locked each and every bolt.

"The light switch is here," he said as he ran one hand across the entrance hallway's wall. "Are you ready?"

"Yeah."

Ellis flicked the switch and hung his jacket, then removed Tiberius' harness. "Good boy," he told the dog. "Go have a drink."

He headed for the living room and said "Tea?"

"No thanks. I'm fine. What's with all the locks? Have you had crazy people threaten you before?"

Ellis turned on the living room lights, then walked to his armchair and sat. "It's to stop anyone getting in during the day."

"And... that's the deal with the curtains, right?" Randall's boots were soft against the carpet, then the sofa groaned quietly as he sat down. "Everything's to keep the sun out."

"Aye." Ellis tugged his glasses off and placed them on the small table to his right. Dreary grey-white light came into his eyes, but he didn't try to focus on anything. It was exhausting, and not usually worth the effort. "I've no proof that sunlight's dangerous, but who wants to stick their hand in a vat of acid on the off-chance it might be the weak stuff? That'd be pretty embarrassing."

"The weak stuff?" Randall echoed.

"Eh, I'm not a scientist." Ellis chuckled. "Anyway. You had questions. Might as well ask 'em."

Randall fidgeted, causing his clothes to rustle together and the leather of the sofa squeak weakly. "How long have you been a vampire?"

His heart was still running fast. Fear, perhaps? That would make sense. Ellis had confessed to being a vampire, then locked Randall in a flat with him. That was probably a bit frightening.

"Under a year," Ellis said. To save Randall the trouble of asking, he continued, "When I was diagnosed with RP I had to undergo further tests. There are different diseases, they all just get referred to as RP as a group, so they wanted to identify which one I had. Anyway, they worked out I had maybe three years of eyesight left." He shrugged. "I carried on. I had a business to run, and I had to work out how the hell I was going to keep it going when I couldn't see. So anyway, Han was a regular customer back then, and I got on pretty well with his PA, Jay, and Jay suggested he come work for me instead. That way he could learn everything while I could still see to teach him, and then once I was totally blind I could rely on him for pretty important decisions. I resisted a while, but Han insisted it was a good idea, and I was wasting time, so I took him on."

"Uh huh." To his credit Randall didn't demand to know where this was going. He listened instead.

Ellis gave a small, bitter smile. "I was blind in two years. I could just about tell whether it was light or dark, but that was it. The doctors all thought it would take longer, but it didn't. I closed the gallery for a while and sent Jay off to be with Han. They'd married by then." He laced his fingers together in his lap and rested his elbows on the arms of his chair. "I couldn't cope. I'd tried to learn braille once I knew I would be blind, but I couldn't read it. Turns out you pretty much have to be blind from birth to have the sensitivity required. Once you've learned to be dependent on your eyesight, your other senses take a back seat as far as development's concerned. So once the gallery was closed I spent about a week getting totally rat-arsed. I didn't even bother to take Tiberius with me, I just went off with a cane so that he didn't have to put up with the late nights." He laughed briefly at the irony. "I got drunk, I flirted, you know. The usual self-destructive spiral. And I met Jonas, who showered me with compliments and acted like I was the sexiest thing he'd ever seen. We got busy, then the damn idiot turned me before we even got to the good bit." Ellis snorted. "Maybe it would've been rubbish. He said he wanted to 'preserve the integrity of an artistic soul'. That's the kind of crap he was full of." He sighed.

Randall had stopped fidgeting. "Why do you call him an idiot?"

"He had no idea I was blind." Ellis laughed again, feeling light-headed. God, he was telling a near-stranger everything about himself. The Council would kill them all for this. "He thought the glasses were a fashion statement and I bumped into everything because I was drunk."

"What about the cane?"

"Aye. Like I said. Idiot. He dragged me off before I could grab it, and I was too pickled to complain. It got left in the pub."

"When you say he turned you-" Randall hesitated.

"Into a vampire. You take all of someone's blood out, then once they're dead you give them some of your own. You've got about a minute after their heart stops or it doesn't work, and if you give them blood before the heart stops it doesn't work then, either. I'm amazed he managed to get it right."

"And by 'take it all out' you mean drink it all, yeah?"

"Aye." Ellis pressed his lips together and tried to push away the memory of Jonas doing just that.

"And you have to drink blood to survive?"

Ellis cracked his knuckles slightly. "Yes."

"Where from?"

The question hung in the air, poised with potential. Two words, but they broached a complex subject laden with the opportunity to upset and offend.

What Randall really wanted to know was whether Ellis was a killer. Which, of course, he was.

"It has to be a living creature," Ellis said, speaking quietly. "Blood already removed from someone or something doesn't work. It's inedible, like food or drink. We have to feed directly from something that's alive when we do so."

"Where," Randall said slowly, "from."

Ellis pushed a hand through his hair. "For god's sake, where do you think? People, Randall. There. Are you happy? I have to feed on people. I don't stand a chance of catching any wild animals in London."

"And what do you do, eh? You bring them home for sex, then kill them? Is that how you do it? Is that what you were going to do to me?" Randall's anger was quick and easy, and Ellis wasn't sure he could deflate it so easily a second time around.

"No. That's not how I do it. I don't kill anyone. I don't need much at all. The older you get the more you need, but I'm young. A few drops every few weeks is enough, unless I get injured."

"Then how do you get it? How do you go unnoticed while you drink blood and bite people-" Randall paused. "You do bite them, right? Or is that bullshit?"

Ellis ran the tip of his tongue along his teeth, then forced his fangs to descend. His gums itched for a moment as his canines grew and sharpened until they could slice skin without any effort, and he bared his teeth and opened his mouth. He drew his lips back.

He felt like a total lemon. His fangs weren't for display, and even bringing them out seemed to prime his body to feed; a slender thread of desire, of hunger, wound itself around his thoughts.

He heard Randall's hiss. The man was afraid again: his heartbeat had picked up where it had been almost back to normal moments before.

Ellis withdrew his fangs and closed his mouth so he wasn't sitting there like some sort of freakish human piranha. "Yes. I bite them."

"Fuck," Randall whispered.

"No. I don't do that. A few kisses, maybe. A bite. Then that's that. I leave."

"Doesn't someone *notice*?"

"It causes pleasure and leaves them dizzy, like all the best kisses should. I make sure they're safe, then I go. There's no mark, no evidence. Maybe a bruise, I don't know, but so long as we breathe on the wound itself it heals too quickly for them to ever see."

"Are you going to kill me?"

Ellis blinked slowly. "Eh?"

"You're telling me everything. Is it 'cause you're going to kill me?"

Ellis huffed. "You daft bloody apeth. Why would I kill you? I want to get you into bed, not ditch your body in the river." He leaned forward and looked in Randall's direction, struggling to focus on the man who was only a few feet away from him. All he could really make out at this distance was a purplish shirt and brown skin. "You're smart and sexy, kind and patient. You're observant and you're dedicated, and you wouldn't hurt a fly unless there were no other way to handle a situation. There's absolutely no point me evading your questions, because I like you a lot and if I ever want you to like me in return I can't go on without you finding all this out sooner or later. And if some barmpot wants to kill me you better bloody well make sure he doesn't hurt you too. So you promise me, Randall. Promise me that if some nutter throws himself at me, you save yourself and you stay safe and you *live*."

Randall's breathing had become ragged around the edges, and his heart thrummed. "Ellis-"

"No. I won't let anyone get hurt because of me. It's better in the long run to consider myself dead from the moment I met Jonas. Everything since then's just been like an added bonus, a long goodbye. But I'm already dead, Randall. Don't you dare let him touch you."

They sat in silence, and only as the sudden anger left him did Ellis truly realise what he'd said.

SEVENTEEN

RANDALL STOOD and walked away from Ellis. It was too much to take in, like when Preeti had first found him all those years ago; too much information, none of it seemed like it could be true.

Ellis *liked* him.

He puffed out his cheeks and wiped his palms on his jeans as he looked around the flat. He would have expected a flat so close to the centre of London to be a poky little thing, but this place was fairly decent now that he could see it. The walls were creamy white, but the carpets, curtains, and leather chairs were all deep burgundy. There were paintings on the walls: beautiful vistas of rolling hillsides in different styles and colours. The ceiling was high and featured old mouldings and plasterwork Randall had never seen in a private home before. There were oak leaves and acorns, carved right around the edges of the room and gilt-painted.

It was a gorgeous flat, and the owner couldn't see it.

Tiberius had gone to a bed in the corner of the living room and was dozing. Now and then he cracked his eyes open to look over at Randall, then closed them again. The dog was comfortable in Ellis' presence. Nothing about the vampire triggered either Tiberius' instincts or his own.

Ellis sat silent, his eerie blue eyes almost following Randall around the room. Almost. He had stopped trying to see - the look of concentration had gone from his delicate features - so now he was simply waiting. Waiting to see what Randall would say, because he liked Randall, and the way he'd said it didn't mean 'as a friend'.

The way Ellis said it made Randall's insides clench with need.

He gazed across the room at Ellis, who remained quiet. Resigned. He looked like a man waiting to be hanged. Did he want to die?

How could this be right? Someone wanted to kill Ellis for what he was. Hell, Briar wanted him dead without even understanding anything about the situation; he'd decided that anything that fed off the blood of living creatures was a parasite that had to be destroyed and that was the end of it, but *everything* lived off something else. That was just nature. It wasn't possible for energy to come from nowhere, and that was the very definition of a food chain. Randall wasn't a vegetarian, and nor were any of his pack. They depended on the death of living creatures to survive, but all Ellis took was a little. Nothing the body couldn't replenish.

Ellis wasn't a killer, either, but half the werewolves Randall knew had killed during their change. Randall had been lucky; Preeti saved him from a fate that she herself hadn't avoided. Both Briar and Preeti had worked for years to find young wolves on the verge of change because they hadn't had anyone to stop them when they'd gone through it alone. Unaided. Unprotected. Unprepared. They'd had to discover what they were and live with the consequences.

In any sane man's eyes that made them monsters.

Ellis had the ability to survive without killing a bloody thing, so didn't that make him *less* of a monster?

Randall ran a hand over his close-cropped hair and thought back to the painting. What kind of vampire hunter would pick on the blind one, anyway? A coward? Someone who was getting trained up by an older, harder hunter and had been pointed toward Ellis like the vampire came with training wheels? And why send a death threat to a vampire who couldn't see it?

He stopped his pacing, and Ellis frowned slowly.

"What is it?"

"This guy knows you're a vampire, and he sends a painting as a threat. But if he knows you enough to know what you are, he must know that you're blind."

Ellis nodded slightly. "He was able to make several detailed sketches of me without me noticing. I'd say he's aware, aye."

"He sends a painting to your office. So either he doesn't care who else finds out, or he thinks Jay already knows."

Ellis' body stiffened, and he stood quickly, walking unerringly toward the hallway. He returned moments later with his phone and braille display.

"What're you doing?"

"If this person knows about Jay, Jay could be in danger. I need to text him-"

Randall couldn't help but grin briefly. With his own existence threatened, Ellis' concern was for everyone living around him. "I don't know if it's wise."

Ellis sat again and placed his phone on the table beside his glasses. "Why not?"

"Jay's gone home and he'll be in Paris tomorrow. If he's a target he's going to be out of reach for a few days, and hopefully we'll have fixed this before he gets home."

Ellis pursed his lips while he thought about that.

He didn't seem to breathe at all while he wasn't speaking. It was eerie now that Randall had noticed it. All these little clues were right there in front of him, but it was becoming easier to understand how a vampire could pass through the millions of people in London without ever being spotted by his prey. Londoners didn't even like to look at each other if they could help it; scrutinising a stranger on the off-chance that he wasn't breathing or didn't have a reflection was totally off the menu.

"That makes sense," Ellis said, and put the reader aside. "But I don't know how we're supposed to stop this fella."

"Can you describe him to me?" Randall went back to the couch and lowered himself to the leather. He rested his elbows on his knees and watched Ellis as he spoke.

Ellis' eyes flitted to the side, and he absently squeezed the arms of his chair. "I couldn't tell you how tall he was," he began, his voice distant as his concentration went elsewhere. "The room was dark, and he would have adjusted the easel to his own height. I wouldn't say he's particularly short, though. The brushes were long-handled. He didn't make an underpainting, he went straight from sketch to finished piece. He's accomplished, but I don't recognise his style. He could be an amateur, or commercially unsuccessful." He had to pause for breath, and he absently pushed hair back from his forehead. "No distinguishing features, no scars or birthmarks that I could see. His hair's brown, medium ash as far as I could tell. His eyes are dark blue. Pthalo blue. He's around Jay's age, maybe mid-twenties. White, perhaps Eastern European. Short-skulled, heart-shaped face. Strong nose, long and straight. Thin lips. Clean-shaven."

Randall stared at him. "You got all that from a vision?"

Ellis shrugged. "I trained as an artist. I might have been rubbish at making decent paintings, but not at observation."

"Apparently not." Randall smiled a little. "Okay. He knows you don't show up on camera. He knows you're a vampire. Either he knows Jay knows what you are, or he knows that you can see things if you touch them. Who knows you can do that?"

Ellis shook his head faintly. "It's impossible to say. I mean, Jay knows, but there's no way of guessing who Jonas ever told."

"Can we ask him?"

Ellis shifted slightly. "No."

Randall bit his cheek. "Is he dead?"

"Aye."

"Bollocks."

Ellis ran fingers over the deep red leather arms of his seat, then said slowly, "I met someone couple of weeks ago, in St. James' Park. Tiberius growled at him the whole time we spoke. Then on Monday in Green Park there was a camera, and then this fella was there again. Tiberius still growled at him, didn't like him at all. He walked with me to the gallery, all the way to the door." He groaned and pinched the bridge of his nose. "It has to be him. Once he was gone, Tiberius was right as rain again."

"And if all Tiberius has been doing the whole time is trying to protect you," Randall concluded, "then it makes sense this is the guy he's tried to lead you away from every time he smelled him."

"Smelled?"

"Yeah. Dogs recognise people by scent way ahead of seeing them. Their sense of smell is staggering."

Ellis bit the inside of his cheek idly. "Barnes," he finally said, as though he were dredging the name up from the bottom of the ocean. "He said his name was Peter Barnes."

"How did the painting get to you?"

"We have occasional deliveries. It came in with today's. Jay doesn't open them until the evening, but it probably came in around noon."

Randall nodded. "Your stuff comes in by courier or something?"

"Oh, aye. Everything's couriered in, for the insurance."

"Then there'll be, like, a note or an invoice or something?"

Ellis broke into a slow grin. "With the originator's name and address. Yes, there should be."

"All right." Randall bit his lip.

Ellis had been honest with him. He'd straight-up admitted what he was, and explained far more than he'd likely wanted to. Was that because he cared about Randall? He'd said that it was information that would have to come out sooner or later if they were ever going to go forward together. They'd both been skipping over that part, but it was there like the elephant in the room, the fact that they danced around and pretended hadn't been laid bare.

There could be a relationship here, and Ellis needed honesty. He had to tell Randall what he was, because he liked Randall, cared for him, would rather die than let anyone hurt him. How could Randall possibly stand here and judge Ellis on anything he'd admitted to when he himself was sitting on a stonking massive secret of his own?

Christ, what would Ellis think of him if he knew? What would Briar do if he found out that not only had Randall not killed Ellis, but also told him what he was? 'Cause he would have to, wouldn't he? He'd leapt in to volunteer, to be the one by Ellis' side through all this stuff, but he wasn't a trained ninja assassin or anything like that. Everything he'd learned in the thirteen years since his change was how *not* to get hurt in a fight; how to take his lumps without getting his throat torn out.

What if he was looking at this all wrong? Barnes wanted Ellis dead, but what if violence wasn't the solution? If he could pick Barnes' scent up off the painting then head to the address it came from they could find the artist and talk to him; try to find out why he was so angry, and how he knew about Ellis.

There could be a peaceful solution.

That all came down to Ellis' reaction to what Randall would have to tell him for them to get that far, wouldn't it?

"What are you thinking?" Ellis asked softly.

"I think we should go back to the gallery." Randall scratched his scalp and bit his lip.

"To find the address."

"Yeah."

Ellis sucked his teeth a moment, then sighed. "Now?"

"I think the quicker we act the better, yeah." Randall nodded.

Now all he had to do was tell Ellis what he was, sniff a painting, and track down a man whose clear intention was to kill the man he was beginning to fall in love with.

Simple.

EIGHTEEN

ELLIS' mood wasn't in any danger of getting better. They were tucked safely away in what was probably one of the most well-defended flats in the entirety of Mayfair and now Randall wanted to *leave* it again?

No. No, no, not in a million years no. They should stay here, where he could hold onto Randall and never let him go.

He felt his teeth with his tongue, then gnawed on his lower lip.

"We could stay here," he suggested.

Randall's pulse didn't respond. His mind wasn't on flirting right now, it seemed. "But the painting itself might have some clues, too."

Ellis grimaced. "You're Hercule Poirot now?"

"No." Now Randall's pulse perked up, and his breathing faltered.

Ellis tilted his head as he tried to work out what was happening. It wasn't arousal, alas. Could it be fear? Stress? What about Ellis' question could have set this off?

"No, I'm not... a detective or anything." Randall swallowed. "I, er."

He straightened in his chair again and waited. Whatever Randall was building up to, an interruption could well make him clam up.

"I'm a werewolf."

Ellis blinked. He felt the urge to laugh, but Randall's breathing was hushed now.

God, he was serious.

"A werewolf," Ellis said slowly.

"Yeah."

"Bollocks," Ellis grumbled. "This isn't funny, Randall. There's no such-" He stopped himself and huffed. "Okay, no. You know what? I'm going to shut up, and you are going to talk."

Randall groaned. "There isn't much more to it than that."

"You can turn into a *wolf!* That's not something you get away with fobbing off." Ellis huffed and grabbed his glasses. He slid them on to cut out the light, because the temptation to try and read Randall's expression was too great and the effort would aggravate him further. With his world reduced to darkness once more, he leaned back in his chair and rested his head against it. He closed his eyes. "From the top," he murmured once he was calmer. "You must know what questions need answers. Were you born a werewolf?"

"Yeah. It seems to be genetic. Recessive. Neither of my parents are werewolves, and my brother isn't either."

Good. They were getting somewhere. Ellis smiled briefly. "Did your mum pop out a hairy little wolf cub, or what?"

He heard Randall make a soft, choked-off laugh, and smiled a little more, relieved that Randall was beginning to relax.

"No. Nothing like that. I was just, you know, a normal baby. Human, nothing too adorable. A bit short."

Ellis lifted his head from the leather and sat upright to listen. "Go on."

Randall shuffled around on the sofa, then settled again. "I didn't lie before," he said quietly. "I was born in Spitalfields, and I grew up there with my mum and my brother Kieran. Our dad walked out." He took a breath. "Anyway. About a week before my sixteenth birthday I was at a party, and I met this girl there. She was a bit older, and she wouldn't stop sniffing me. It was pretty strange. She said I shouldn't go home that night; that I'd regret it if I did. I'd already figured out I was gay, and I thought she might be trying to chat me up, so I told her I wasn't interested."

Ellis laughed softly into his hand.

Randall huffed. "Yeah, I know. I was fifteen. What do you want?" He chuckled, though. "So I told her no, and she said I was a werewolf, and if I went home that night I'd kill someone. She spoke about the dreams I'd been having like she'd seen them herself, and she knew things I hadn't told anyone."

Ellis lowered his hand and leaned forward. "Bloody hell."

"Yeah. She was so serious, you know? Totally believed what she was saying. I was terrified. If she'd just told me what I was, I wouldn't have believed her. I didn't believe her anyway, but who can risk something like that happening?" Randall paused. "Anyway, I found a phone and called mum to tell her I wouldn't be home that night. Said I'd met a girl at the party and I was going back to her place for the night."

"I bet your mum loved that," Ellis breathed.

Randall laughed. "She chewed my ear off so much I had to hang up in the end. God, she was livid. I went off with this girl and she introduced me to her boyfriend and a couple of other people. All werewolves. And we sat out in Grovelands Park all night, and I changed." Leather creaked slightly, then Randall's boots swished across the carpet. He'd begun to pace again.

"And did you kill anyone?" Ellis asked. He kept his question neutral, knowing full well he didn't have a leg to stand on here.

"No. I wanted to. Well, I didn't *want* to. There was this… anger in me. This rage. I hadn't ever felt anything like it. I was, like, the most placid child known to man and I couldn't deal with it. It came out of nowhere and I just wanted to go out and hunt something living and tear it to pieces and eat the-" Randall's throat closed around his voice, and his breathing shuddered. "There's a thing that only the Alpha of a pack can do. He can talk you down from that. He can keep a whole pack calm during the full moon, and he can keep the wolf from killing when it first emerges. You change, and he's there to bring you back down, and it's such a relief…" Randall tailed off.

"Is it near full moon now? I can't say I keep track of that kind of information."

"Yeah. Very near."

Ellis rubbed his stubble while he ran through small details in his mind. Randall's heartrate had spiked a couple of times earlier in the evening, and his breathing and tone had suggested some seemingly random anger. If Ellis had known he had a werewolf in front of him, would he have attempted to defuse that anger so quickly? Had it been dangerous for him to do so? "You seem fairly calm," he ventured.

"Yeah." Randall seemed surprised. "This close to the full moon, being away from the pack is dangerous."

"For you?"

"For everyone near me. I don't even want to think about what could go wrong."

Ellis nodded to himself. "What is it you can do, then? If you tell me you can't turn into a wolf I'm going to be reet let down."

Randall coughed. "Yeah. I can turn into a wolf." He hesitated. "And, er. Something else."

"Stepney's Man of Mystery," Ellis said dryly. "All or nothing. Out with it."

Randall huffed. "We call it Halfway. It's, um. It's kind of half human, half wolf. But with like the bulk of both."

Ellis squinted as he tried to picture it. "Are we talking your traditional gigantic wolf man with huge claws and bulging muscles?"

"Yeah," Randall said slowly. "Pretty much, yeah. Ten feet tall, heavier than a Siberian tiger, claws like knives, strong enough to tear open a house, that kind of stuff."

Ellis pursed his lips.

"Show me," he said.

Randall coughed. "I'd have to, um, get undressed first."

"In that case I insist." Ellis grinned, and was rewarded with a soft cough from Randall. "I'll help you."

He could hear Randall fidgeting with his shirt. "I don't know," the werewolf said. "With the moon and everything, I might not be, um… I might not be in full control."

Ellis smirked and slid to his feet. He stepped across the room toward Randall's quick, uncertain breaths, and placed his hands on the shorter man's chest. "That doesn't sound so bad," he murmured as he felt the hard muscles beneath soft cotton.

"It sounds fairly bad," Randall squeaked.

"Mmhmm." Ellis found the buttons and began to unfasten them.

It was a gamble, of course. If everything Randall had said was true there was every chance that he could lose control here and tear Ellis' head off or something equally grisly. Yet Randall had come close to anger twice already this evening, and whatever Ellis had done, it brought him straight back down again - something Randall seemed convinced was a kind of mystic power that only Alpha werewolves had.

He had to trust that Randall wouldn't hurt him, otherwise what kind of useless bodyguard would he be? If he could show the wolf here and now that Randall *could* control himself, he might grow a bit more confidence.

Of course, if Ellis was wrong he'd only reinforce Randall's worst fears.

He worked slowly, listening intently to Randall's heart, his breath, the faint whimpers that barely made a sound at the back of his throat. This close he could smell Randall's sweat and deodorant. He moved with deliberate care and kept his touch light and gentle while he unfastened the last of the buttons and murmured "Is this the shirt that you wore last night?"

"Hnnh. Yes." Randall swallowed.

"I thought so." He smiled faintly. "It feels new. Did you buy it for our date?"

"Yeah."

"That's incredibly sweet of you." He leaned in and kissed Randall's shoulder as he peeled the shirt aside and exposed it. "Glad I get to take it off you a second time, then."

He swept his hands down Randall's arms, pushing the shirt's sleeves away until the material was bunched between Randall's wrists. He kissed Randall's shoulder and neck in small, light pecks as he pulled on the shirt until the sleeves were inside-out and he could work them off over Randall's hands. The heat rising from Randall's skin was enticing, and his scent shifted with arousal. It bore a slight woodsy musk, beneath the chemical taste of his deodorant.

Randall's fingers twitched under his touch once he was free of the shirt, and he brought his hands up to Ellis' hips.

Good. Good, he was paying attention. Releasing his fear, even if only a wee bit. Ellis smiled softly and rewarded him with a kiss to his jaw.

He dipped his hands between them and unfastened Randall's trousers. He'd worn trousers again; he'd wanted to make a good impression.

Ah, yes. Ellis had rather promised to screw his brains out tonight, hadn't he? And Randall had come, despite knowing what he was, despite knowing his control was poor this time of the month. Possibly Randall hadn't been thinking all that clearly there, and Ellis couldn't help but feel flattered. Dangerously, terrifyingly flattered.

Apparently he had the power to make this powerful creature forget he could tear people asunder. Was that a good thing?

He unzipped Randall's fly and eased his fingers under the waistband of his briefs, then eased them down over Randall's strong, solid thighs. Briefs and trousers bunched together as Ellis bent his knees and ran his palms further down. He caressed the back of Randall's knees, then his calves, and Randall put his hands on Ellis' shoulders when his legs wobbled.

He unlaced Randall's hiking boots, then helped him step out of everything. Boots, socks, trousers, and briefs, all set aside.

Ellis tipped his head back to face Randall - or probably Randall's chest. His goal wasn't to see. His intention was to give Randall something to look at.

It certainly worked. Randall's fingers tightened on his shoulders, and the stocky man groaned.

Ellis grinned and murmured "Okay. Show me what you've got."

Randall cleared his throat, and made an awkward pleading noise.

"Blow job later," Ellis chuckled. "Once you're human again. Just in case you were having the most bonkers mental image ever just then. Come on, show me."

"You're a tease," Randall growled.

"It has been said. Now get on all fours for me."

Randall made the most adorable sound of protest, but sank to his knees as he was told.

Ellis felt along Randall's arm, then rested a hand on his shoulder and nodded. "Whenever you are ready," he said, dropping the flirtatious hint from his voice.

"Okay." Randall let go of him, and then Ellis heard the most god-awful noises he'd ever encountered emanating from a living creature.

They weren't loud, but they were loud enough. There was wet tearing, and splintering of bone, and grinding of surfaces that probably shouldn't be moving the way that they were. The skin and muscle under his hand rippled unnaturally, and pinpricks burst from the surface before they softened into fur. Thick, dense fur, soft and fluffy.

The pitch of Randall's breathing changed. Now it was more like Tiberius', the shape of his chest and size of his airway producing a wholly different sound.

Ellis brought up his other hand and ran both over Randall's fur.

There was a wolf in his flat.

He laughed weakly. "Oh my god."

Randall sat, and his tail swished against the carpet. He pressed a cold, wet nose against Ellis' cheek.

"Bloody hell." Ellis dug his fingers through the fur until he could find the body beneath. "This is... you. It's really you."

Randall chuffed in agreement. At least, it *sounded* like agreement.

Randall could turn into a wolf. It had only taken a few seconds, and now...

Now Ellis had a cold, creeping sense of terror at what Randall had said he could also turn into.

This was his home, and he had someone in it who could become a massive killing machine.

Here he'd been trying to get Randall into bed. 'Cause the night just wasn't scary enough, apparently.

"All right," he said slowly. "Okay. I'm a vampire, you're a werewolf, and that's all absolutely... fine. Totally okay."

Randall rippled and convulsed beneath his hands, and for a second Ellis felt a stab of fear. Was Randall ill? Had something gone wrong?

His fur withdrew back into his skin, and the grotesque sounds faded as quickly as they'd come. Ellis sagged with relief.

"Yeah." Randall was sheepish. "Anyway. Shall we go to your office?"

Ellis grimaced. "I don't know. I went to a lot of effort to get you naked."

"That's fine. I've got a plan."

Ellis listened as Randall outlined his plan.

It was ridiculous. Ludicrous. Audacious.

He didn't know whether to laugh or give himself over to the insanity with abandon.

NINETEEN

RANDALL HELD his head high and his tail even higher. He was a wolf, and he was walking through the streets of Mayfair without hiding in the shadows or skulking between trees. Normally if he wanted to prowl London in this shape he had to run from one shadow to the next like a fox here to steal from the bins, but tonight?

Tonight, Randall was a guide dog.

Ellis had protested. He'd argued that Randall didn't have any training in being a guide dog, and he was right; Randall didn't have a clue what he was doing. All he knew was what he'd read when he'd done his research on guide dog training, but none of that explained how the harness would convey every movement Ellis made down through his shoulders, or what those movements were supposed to mean - if anything.

The harness was uncomfortable. It was made for Tiberius, and they'd had to alter the fittings to get it around Randall's body. Ellis wasn't happy about that, either.

Randall was dragging the vampire out of his comfort zone, and he didn't feel safe, but Randall had argued that Ellis didn't feel safe right now anyway; not after that painting.

Ellis had dug out Tiberius' reflective winter coat and used it to cover much of Randall's body to hide his decidedly more wolfen shape and fur profile. Then he'd used boot polish to hide the ruddy colouration to Randall's fur.

That was a peculiar experience. They had gone into the spare bedroom, where a full length mirror remained on the inside of a wardrobe door, and Randall had watched as a tin floated around him and black smeared itself over his exposed fur to try to disguise his non-domesticated appearance. Ellis had taken his glasses off and squinted at him at close range while he worked, but nothing of him - not his body and not his clothes - showed in that mirror.

Only the tin he held.

With his full senses, Ellis still had no odour of his own. Randall could pick out the lingering hints of soap and shampoo, toothpaste and mouthwash, but there was no natural scent beneath it all.

Could that be how Barnes had worked out what Ellis was? If Ellis failed to reflect that might go unnoticed, but if whatever he held still showed up then it could draw the eye as unusual, like catching a living statue out of the corner of the eye on the South Bank. It could be something so simple as Tiberius' harness floating along that had betrayed Ellis to this crazy stalker.

Randall had so many more questions to ask Ellis, but this shape wouldn't allow for human communication. He'd have to wait until they got back to the flat.

"Left turn," Ellis said tersely.

Randall numbly realised Ellis had already said it twice, and he rumbled apologetically as he turned.

Ellis huffed. "I didn't know wolves were stone deaf."

I'm not, Randall protested with a flick of his ears, a rumble in his chest. *I wasn't paying attention.*

"You were off in laa-laa land, weren't you?" Ellis tutted. "Come on. If this is going to work you have got to be alert. And don't forget to look up. You'll have to steer me around anything I might walk into whether it's at your height or mine."

Randall began to regret this plan. It had seemed like such a great idea. They could go to the gallery and he'd be able to pick up Barnes' scent from the painting, then detect whether or not it was at the address the art had been couriered in from. If Barnes were close by that address Randall could even lead Ellis to him, and if they could take him by surprise they might be able to scare him off or talk him out of being a psycho. Ellis seemed to be good at talking, so they could be in with a chance.

They'd never get that far if Randall couldn't stop Ellis from twisting his ankle on a crooked piece of pavement, or getting brained by a low-hanging pub sign.

He took a breath and tried to focus on the job at hand.

They made it to the gallery with little more incident, although Randall had to admit that was likely down to Ellis' circuitous, traffic-free route. Ellis unlocked the door and felt his way to the security panel, centring his fingers over the keys before he tapped the code in. Then he closed the front door and headed for the stairs.

"Hand rail to my right," Ellis explained. "That puts you roughly in the centre of the stairs, I think."

Randall adjusted his course slightly. He had indeed been about to walk up the left-hand edge of the stairs, which would have left Ellis in the middle of nowhere.

"Thank you," Ellis murmured when his hand touched the rail.

They reached the office, where Ellis turned the lights on, and added "Where did Jay put it?"

Randall looked toward the neat stack of paintings in a rack and hoped that was where Jay had ditched it. He moved forward slowly to give Ellis time to adjust to the movement and nosed through the stack until he found the only unwrapped one. It had Jay's scent on it, as well as some other, so he gently gripped it in his teeth and tugged it free.

The image was just as horrible as it had been earlier in the evening.

"Got it?"

Rrr, Randall answered.

"All right. Let me know when you're done." Ellis lowered the harness' handle to rest against Randall's back and released it, then stepped away, one hand trailing along the wall until he found his desk. He sat, facing Randall, and waited.

Scent was like colour to him in this shape, replacing the lost reds and greens with swirls of information that settled in layers and told him not only where something had been, but also how long ago and how quickly it had moved. If it was a living thing he could usually detect whether it had been calm or agitated. There was so much data that humans were surrounded by yet utterly unaware of that it had taken him years to master the view of the world from his nose.

He ran his tongue over the finely-tuned organ to enhance his sense, then began to examine the painting close up.

It smelled faintly of plastic, but the majority of odours daubed across it were at the edges rather than the painting itself. Fingerprints bright as day were the freshest, and the scent was certainly Jay's; it matched the odours from the other desk in the room perfectly. There were other prints, dimmer and older, and not from a person he recognised. The paint overlapped them here and there, where brush strokes had gone beyond the edge of the canvas, and Randall sniffed each and every one that he found to familiarise himself with the unique flavour lingering after those fleeting touches.

The scent was human, and so far as Randall could tell the owner kept his hands clean. There were no traces of food or mess in those fingerprints.

He did his best to memorise the odour, then he nosed the canvas back in among the others.

"Are you done?" Ellis murmured.

Rrrf.

"Okay. There should be a shipping manifest somewhere. If Jay's opened it, it'll be a couple of pieces of A4 paper with today's date and a list of the paintings that came in. There were only two in today's delivery, so you're looking for a courier's letterhead, two line items, today's date, and the second page is just information about insurance and making claims, that sort of midden."

Randall snorted. It seemed the more relaxed - or stressed - Ellis got, the more the Yorkshire oozed out of him.

"Aye, laugh away, furboy. And when yer done we'll get you home and give you a reet good shaving. I doubt Jay's had the time to file it away, so it should be near those paintings, I'll 'appen."

Randall followed the trail of Jay's scent. It was everywhere in the office, but he stuck with the painting and the layer of time that matched Jay's fingerprints there; no more than a couple of hours old. The trail spread from the office door to Ellis' desk, across the desk, back to where the painting stood... He followed it, retracing every single step Jay took until he found a sealed envelope on Jay's desk, neatly resting on the top of his intray. He had to stand with his paws on the desk to reach it, and nosed it out of the tray until he could see it. It had a courier's label instead of a postage stamp, and the date matched.

He took it carefully in his teeth and held his tongue back to stop it getting too wet, then sprinted to Ellis and pressed the envelope against his hand.

"What-" Ellis felt the envelope, then nodded. "Ah. He hasn't opened it, eh? Right."

Ellis' thumb found the flap, and he teased the envelope open, only tearing it in a couple of places. His hand dipped inside and he drew out sheafs of folded paper. He tossed the empty envelope onto his desk and unfolded the sheets, then held them up toward Randall. "Is this it?"

Randall's gaze flit over the page. It was upside down, but he couldn't work out how to tell Ellis that, so he tilted his head and said *Rrr*.

"Good. Can you read it?"

Hrr.

Ellis nodded and remained still, patient as a rock.

The manifest showed two paintings, but it was the second which struck Randall as more important right now.

The Parasite's End. Barnes, Peter. Acrylic on Canvas. Unvarnished.

He growled, and Ellis' grip on the paper tightened.

"Randall?"

He nudged his nose against Ellis' hand by way of apology and squinted at the address. Queen Anne's Gate, London. He didn't have a clue where that was, but it was an SW1 postcode so couldn't be far.

Ellis took one hand from the paper and patted the top of Randall's head, then grimaced when he felt the boot polish. "Buggering hell. I forgot about that. Did you get the address?"

Yes, but I don't know where it is. Randall chuffed and flicked his tail in frustration.

"Is it a London postcode?"

Randall nodded. *Yes.*

"Central?"

Randall's tail thumped. *Yes.* God, Ellis was brilliant!

"North?"

Ellis cycled through every cardinal direction there was until

Randall had given an affirmative sound to both South and West, then Ellis began at the top with "One?"

Rrr!

"SW1?"

Rrr!

"Bollocks." Ellis sighed and set the paper on his desk.

Randall tipped his head and his tail stilled. *What? What is it?*

"Outside of my territory," Ellis said. "That's Westminster. Is it SW1Y?" He sounded hopeful.

No. Randall grumbled an apology.

Ellis bit his lip while he thought, then nodded a little. "SW1A?"

No.

"Urgh. God, what else is down there. SW1H?"

Yes! Randall's tail thumped and he nudged Ellis' hand again.

Ellis sucked his teeth. "That's... Petty France, Broadway, New Scotland Yard... Just south of St. James' Park. Do you know how to get there?"

Yes! Randall nodded.

"Okay." Ellis didn't look too convinced, but he pointed to the floor to his left. "Can you come here and face forward please?"

Randall understood. Ellis wanted him in the position he'd normally find Tiberius. He obliged, and let out a small rumble once he was in place.

Ellis felt along the fluorescent coat until he found the harness' handle, and he stood. "Right. I don't know St. James' Park too well, but there's a sort of lake in the middle of it with a bridge that goes over the water. I don't know whether the water's safe, so I want to go around the lake until we meet up with that bridge on the south side. Then if I remember right the path from the bridge goes straight to the edge of the park, and we can sneak over the road there and down Queen Anne's Gate into-"

Randall yipped. *Yes! Yes, that's it! That's the place!*

"Queen Anne's Gate?" Ellis repeated with care.

Yes!

Ellis puffed out his cheeks, then nodded. "Right. Let's go. But if you find any other vampires we are going to run like our arses are on fire, got it?"

Randall nodded. *Yes.*

He might not understand vampires, but he was more than familiar with the concept of territory.

"Go. And let me stop at the door to alarm the place before we go."

Yes.

Randall led Ellis from the office, and waited for him to touch the handrail before they descended the stairs.

TWENTY

Ellis gripped Tiberius' harness too tightly. He couldn't help it, and it probably wasn't helping Randall at all, but he was bloody terrified.

He was about to invade someone else's territory for no damn good reason, just because a mortal artist happened to have sent him a painting from an address beyond his own boundaries. If he got caught and the situation went horribly wrong he could be destroyed and it would be completely legal. There was no reason for his presence to be tolerated in the slightest.

It was the law which had tolerated Ellis' destruction of Jonas, after all. Ellis had told his story, there was no evidence to the contrary; case closed. The Council was notified, the Constabulary investigated the death, and in the end Ellis had gotten off with a polite thank you and no further repercussions.

Really all you had to do to kill another vampire was make sure they'd crossed the boundaries into your turf first.

He directed Randall as far as Green Park, leading him in through Constitution Hill so that they could beeline straight toward The Mall and cross into St. James' Park as far away from Buckingham Palace as possible. From there on it would have to be down to Randall to navigate.

Why would Barnes go to the trouble of sending Ellis a painting? Why even go so far as to create a work of art? It seemed a hell of a lot of effort to go to if killing Ellis was Barnes' goal. What stopped Barnes from simply jumping Ellis without warning one night? Barnes knew where Ellis walked his dog, he knew where he worked. He had probably even stalked Ellis to the front door of his flats at one point.

Was there some other motive at work? More than simple murder, more than the destruction of something or someone that Barnes clearly loathed?

He idly bit the inside of his cheek as they walked. Barnes was an artist. His style was effective, a good example of naïve art. Had he trained in naïveté, or was he genuinely self-taught? Could he be a frustrated artist, angry that his work hadn't achieved commercial success?

Had Ellis declined to represent him at the gallery?

He didn't think so, but if he had it might explain Barnes' loathing to some degree. It didn't go anywhere near how Barnes knew what he was, though, or why he'd go so far to get such a hate-filled death threat into his hands.

Ellis swore softly.

It all came back to the fact that Barnes knew he was a vampire.

Did he know what Ellis' power was, too? How could he *possibly* know that?

"Rroo?" Randall asked.

"It's okay," Ellis muttered. "I'm just trying to work out what the hell Barnes gets out of bothering with a painting."

"Rrr," Randall replied, as though he agreed. Then he growled so savagely that for a moment Ellis thought they were about to get attacked - until the growl ended with an upward lilt.

A question.

A growl as a question. Context. The context was what Barnes might get out of...

Ellis blinked. "Fear?"

"Rr!" He heard Randall's tail swish as it wagged.

"He creates *fear*. That's what he gets. It's terrorism." Ellis ran his tongue along his teeth so hard that he almost cut into it. "He wants me to be afraid."

"Hrr!"

"You're a damn genius, Randall." Ellis tried to relax his grip on the harness slightly. He'd had years of getting shoved around by his brothers, and he bloody well wasn't going to let a total stranger do it to him. "Oh." He hesitated as an idea struck him. "Shit."

"Roo?"

"He *knows*," Ellis hissed. "He knows. Who I am, what I am, where I am, what I can do."

"Urr-hhhh…"

Jonas knew all of this. Jonas who had turned Ellis and taught him how to survive, before he summarily lost interest like he had more important things to do.

Had Barnes been that more important thing?

Ellis groaned. Had he killed Barnes' lover?

If that were the case, how did Barnes ever find out? Had Jonas told Barnes about Ellis? Had he revealed Ellis' power and his gallery's address? Jonas could spin a story that would turn the most innocent action into a sign that the end was nigh. Was it possible he'd spent his time with Barnes complaining about Ellis' existence, or how Ellis had 'tricked' him into not knowing that he was blind? Could he have confided in Barnes and confessed his true nature while wishing that he'd never turned Ellis so that he could turn Barnes instead?

Jonas had been in love with art and artists. He'd wanted to preserve Ellis' artistic nature like it could be kept on display for all time. When he realised Ellis wasn't an artist and couldn't damn well see a thing he'd been furious.

He had the permission of the Council to create a fledgling, but he'd chosen poorly, and now their quota was full. They wouldn't allow another to be created, especially by the same vampire. It would have been a political uproar. But if Jonas' fledgling got destroyed he might have been able to petition the Council for permission to turn a replacement.

Ellis had no idea whether they would have allowed it, but they may have if Jonas had hammed up Ellis' blindness and insisted that he hadn't released Ellis into adulthood yet. To lose a fledgling while still under his care might be considered a special circumstance.

Was that why Jonas had come to him that night, full of hatred and ready to kill him in his own gallery? Was that what it had all been about?

Did Jonas want to destroy him so that he could turn Barnes instead?

"I don't know," he answered Randall, his brain still ticking over on it. "I'm wondering if Barnes was Jonas' lover, but if Barnes is looking for revenge what's taken him so long? If Jonas told Barnes where he was going when he came to attack me, surely Barnes would've sussed it out straight away?"

"Hrr," Randall agreed. At least, that's what Ellis decided he did. It was like talking to Tiberius: it felt like a conversation, but in reality it was all taking place in Ellis' head.

Well, that wasn't strictly true. Randall *was* a werewolf. He was intelligent, and he was clearly still every bit as smart while on four legs as he was on two. It was more like the fantasy of two-way communication that most dog owners liked to think they had, but with some meat on the gristle.

"There's something we're missing," Ellis grumbled. "There has to be. It doesn't line up right. Maybe Barnes was incarcerated and only just got out?"

"Urr," Randall said in a tone that somehow conveyed *maybe*.

Ellis bit the tip of his tongue and stopped talking. Words were coming out now without any thought behind them at all, so the best thing to do was nip that right in the bud. Besides, Barnes had found him in this park before; what if he were here again, and found Ellis wandering along talking to his dog?

They walked together toward the lake at the centre of the park, and then Randall cut across him, turning right so abruptly that Ellis walked into him and grabbed at the wolf's back to keep himself from falling over. "Bollocks!"

"Haruu," Randall said, sounding contrite. *Sorry.*

"It's fine. It's my fault." Ellis crouched to check that he hadn't wrenched the harness out of place, then he straightened Randall's jacket. "Are we at the bridge?"

"Uff."

Ellis nodded warily and remained crouched as he listened.

There.

A gentle lap of water against the bank. Nothing violent, no crashing of waves or splashing of a current. The slight breeze was all that caused an occasional gentle *slurp* against the edges of the lake.

Ellis wished he could remember whether the lake were natural or artificial, but this was outside his territory and he - usually - had absolutely no cause to be here. It was pointless memorising every feature of a place he wasn't allowed to be.

It didn't sound like running water. It sounded static.

He puffed out his cheeks and considered the bridge. It would save them a good quarter of an hour or so to use it, and it prevented them from going near the Palace, but dear god if he was wrong about it not being running water he'd be screwed.

Unless Jonas had made all that up too.

"Randall," he said cautiously.

"Rr?"

"Can you see the water?"

"Hrr."

He nodded faintly. "Is it running, like a river?"

Randall's body moved slightly, then he said "Uoo."

"So it's still water?"

"Hrr!"

Bugger it. They didn't have all night.

"Okay. We're going to try the bridge. But for god's sake if anything goes wrong, drag me off it with your damn teeth if you have to, right?"

"Hrruuuu?!"

Ellis shook his head. "It'll add half an hour, at least, just to go around the lake the long way in both directions, and if we get further into Westminster and have to run for it, it'd be nice to know whether using this bridge for an escape route would be remotely possible. If we try it now when there's nobody around it's better than getting forced into it later and finding out it's a disaster. It's not running water; it *should* be okay."

He hoped.

"Hrr," Randall said, still sounding uncertain.

"Okay." Ellis straightened up and took the harness in hand, then said the words he fervently prayed wouldn't kill him. "To the bridge. Carefully."

Randall chuffed and turned left, and Ellis walked alongside him listening desperately for any indication that this was a terrible mistake: rushing water, witnesses, hate-filled artists with an axe to grind.

The surface underfoot changed, and the transition from gravel path to damp wood was immediate.

"Roo?"

"It's fine. It's okay. Keep going."

Randall's claws scraped dully over the wooden bridge, and Ellis' shoes sounded like the trudging of a condemned man. It seemed to go on, and on, and he began to wonder if this was what happened: if you became trapped, forever crossing the bridge, never knowing that you weren't going anywhere. That couldn't happen, could it? Jonas said crossing running water drove a vampire insane, that it killed more fledglings every year than violence or starvation or accidents. He said once the water had you, you never came back.

"Arruuhh!" Randall chuffed.

Ellis heard gravel crunch underfoot, and laughed with relief.

"Oh god. We made it?"

"Rrf," said Randall, sounding completely bemused.

Suddenly Ellis had a lot more sympathy for Randall's fears about the full moon.

"Bloody hell. You're tremendous, Randall. You really are. Let's crack on."

Randall made some sort of sound that sounded like it could be laughter. Or Muttley. He could've turned into Muttley.

Ellis blew a raspberry at him. "Come on. I think this park shuts at midnight or something ridiculous like that. If we're to come back this way at all we need to get a wiggle on."

"Hrr!"

Randall began to move, and Ellis hurried along beside him until the gravel turned to pavement, and the pavement gave way to the knobbled surface that indicated a pedestrian crossing.

Get in, get out. It would be quick, simple, and nobody ever needed to know they were here.

Ellis nodded, and they crossed the road.

TWENTY-ONE

RANDALL COULDN'T BEGIN to wonder what all the fuss about the bridge had been. Was it true, then, that vampires couldn't cross running water? Ellis had seemed about ready to mess himself by the time they'd ended the terrible ordeal of using a short, wide, perfectly safe bridge. What had he thought could happen?

There'd been pretty nice views from that bridge, too. Randall had been able to make out the lights of the London Eye beyond the lake and trees, sparkling in the night sky and lit up in colours he could only half-see.

He crossed the road and approached a tall set of black iron gates which blocked their way, but thankfully there were smaller gates to either side which were held open by bulky, padlocked chains. The smaller gates would be barely wide enough for him and Ellis to pass through side by side, so he slowed down when they reached the narrow portals and crammed his body up against the post on his left as he carefully eased Ellis through the gap.

Ellis tipped his head to one side, then nudged the other post with his elbow and gave a slight nod of understanding.

Once they were through, Randall continued along the ancient, cracked pavement and weaved around any bumps which he thought could trip Ellis.

Being a guide dog was bloody hard work.

The road opened out into a street which faced St. James' Park tube station. To Randall's right was a vast and ugly concrete building that looked like it had been designed in the 1970's, but the road continued to his left in a wide yet quiet street lined with ornately carved porches and iron railings. The road all but reeked of old money, and the parking bays were filled with new Land Rovers, Mercedes', and BMW's.

He took a gamble that they weren't here for the hideous lump of concrete and turned left, his gaze searching for house numbers on every door that they passed.

The buildings were far beyond anything Randall could imagine being able to afford. Five storeys plus the tell-tale subterranean windows of a basement, each terraced house was similar to the next, yet unique in the details. There were small and ornate stone carvings over each arched window, and far more complex and beautiful carved wooden porches overhanging the stone steps leading up to each lacquered door. Each porch held a lantern suspended from it that looked as though they had once been gaslight and now were converted to use electricity.

Even the streetlamps were unlike most of the ones Randall was familiar with; tall and elegant, iron with jewel-like lanterns at the top. They were short, too; presumably so that a man with a stick could light them a hundred or so years ago.

He let out a low rumble of appreciation, then noticed he was on the wrong side of the road. He had evens to his left, so the odd numbers had to be across the street, and he carefully nudged Ellis to the kerb and stopped.

"Is this it?" Ellis breathed.

No. Randall grumbled softly. He nosed Ellis' ankle, then moved forward a couple of inches.

Ellis stepped forward, then paused at Randall's slight rumble. He seemed to understand at the last moment, and felt carefully with his toes until he found the lower road surface.

"God, this is like a bloody lottery," Ellis muttered. "We didn't think this through, did we?"

No, Randall agreed, chuckling softly.

He led Ellis across the street and paused again for him to step up the opposite kerb and back onto pavement, then he drew Ellis toward the faintest whiff of a familiar scent.

Barnes had been here. Not tonight, not recently, but certainly about two weeks ago. His aroma was almost gone, washed away by subsequent rains and a myriad of people passing through during daylight hours, but Randall stepped towards one of the houses set back from the street and caught a stronger touch of it lingering on the old brass door knob.

He nudged Ellis' ankle to warn him of the doorstep, then sat down once they were both on it.

"*This* is it?" Ellis whispered.

"Hrrff," Randall answered.

"Is Barnes here?"

"Uhroo." He chuffed in frustration.

What the hell were they doing here?

Randall had been so wrapped up in proving himself useful, in desperately wanting to save Ellis' life, that he hadn't spared a thought for what they were going to do once they arrived at the courier's address. There was a small plaque beside the door that confirmed the company's name, matched the logo on their letterhead, but the door was shut and it was late at night. If this house had been converted to offices there wouldn't be anyone here.

He glanced to the side of the door and down into the pit alongside the basement windows. Could they break in? They'd be out of sight down there while they tried, but if the owners had any sense at all the place would have some kind of security, and Randall was hardly a burglar.

"I can't say as I've ever done a B&E before," Ellis muttered, somehow echoing Randall's thoughts. "If they have cameras in there I wouldn't show up, but I haven't the foggiest about the layout in there. It'd be like trying to find a needle in a haystack, except I'd actually stand a chance of finding a bloody needle in an actual haystack."

Randall rumbled in agreement.

"Bugger," Ellis groused. "We are the worst burglars ever. Barnes' address has to be in here somewhere, and it might as well be in Atlantis for all the good it's doing us." He flexed the fingers of his right hand as it hung by his side.

Randall agreed again. If they entered the offices, Randall would have to take human form to help with the search. Hell, he'd be the one *doing* the search. CCTV would get them both utterly screwed unless they also managed to find where it was being recorded and pinch the drives the data was written to.

Computers weren't really Randall's thing. He didn't hold out much hope of success in finding the right devices or storage. Besides, they probably would have tripped an alarm just by getting in there in the first place.

He huffed, frustrated. They'd gone to a place that was probably some other vampire's territory without thinking first, and now they were faced with the awesome power of a single locked door, and they were utterly stumped by it.

Randall laughed weakly.

Ellis tipped his head toward Randall, then chuckled. "Shut up. It was your idea." Then he bit his lip. "And mine. Okay, it was *our* idea, and it was ridiculous. At least we've confirmed that Barnes was here, aye?"

"Rrf," Randall agreed.

"Right. Let's pretend that's good enough and well worth the risk." Ellis backed off the step, and Randall wriggled alongside him in reverse. "If I give you my keys in the morning, you could pop to the gallery and snag the paperwork, and we can find out whether these people are open on Sundays."

"Howwrrr?" Randall began to lead Ellis back toward the iron gates at the bend in the road.

"If not we'll have to wait until Monday," Ellis explained. "Then you can call them and say that we need to contact whomever sent us the consignment today as they didn't include an address. Give them some waffle about how we'd like to represent one of the artists involved and the poor fella could miss out on a lot of money if we can't figure out who he is or how to negotiate with him."

Randall snorted at the idea of blagging personal details like that out of a company in all violation of the Data Protection Act.

Ellis tutted. "Well, Jay could do it," he said.

Randall swiveled his eyes up to regard Ellis.

Did the vampire actually *understand* him?

They seemed to be conversing. They'd been doing so the whole way here. At first Randall had found it convenient. Then he'd figured

Ellis just talked to Tiberius a lot as they wandered around the city and was doing much the same thing with Randall.

But the fact was that they genuinely seemed to have some level of comprehension between them. Randall licked his nose, then said *Do you know what I am saying?*

He instantly felt foolish. It was a ridiculous fantasy. Werewolves could understand each other in their various forms, but Ellis wasn't Dr. Doolittle.

"What is it?" Ellis asked.

Randall's tail flagged. *Nothing.*

Ellis nodded a little. "Let's get home and we can talk properly."

"Rrrf," Randall agreed.

He steered Ellis back through the gate with every bit as much care as he had used earlier, and they trudged across Birdcage Walk and into St. James' Park. Ellis seemed lost in thought - or perhaps he was dreading using the bridge again - and Randall tried to figure out if there were some other way they could get Barnes' address. They could have a look online to see whether Barnes had a website. That should probably have been their first step, now that he thought about it.

It had to be the moon. He glanced up to the sky and saw the vast, pale disk between the clouds, so bright that it made them glow with silvery light. She was so very nearly full. Tomorrow night she would reach her peak, but this close was more than enough to make tempers high and bring most of his pack to the edge of violence.

Here he was, though, by Ellis' side. Calm and controlled. He'd come up with an impulsive plan, but if being a bit impulsive was the least of his worries...

Could he survive without a pack? Would he be able to live his life and not suffer the constant, unjustified bullying just so that he had access to Briar's calming influence every month?

Now *there* was a thought. If Ellis had the power to stop Randall losing his temper for three nights a month, what could that mean for him?

It was freedom, pure and simple.

Well, almost freedom. He glanced to Ellis again. There was the small matter of Ellis being a vampire. If Briar ever found out, he'd have Ellis killed.

Hell, he'd probably kill Randall for the betrayal, too.

He hung his head as he walked. They crossed the bridge without incident, and headed back through Green Park, across Piccadilly, and into the warren of Mayfair all without any sign that enemy vampires were in pursuit.

What *were* they going to do if they managed to get Barnes' address? They couldn't get him arrested for sending Ellis a painting; it was only a death threat if you were aware of Ellis' true nature.

If Barnes was intent on killing Ellis, he wouldn't stop after a visit, surely?

Randall's wolf knew the answer to that. That kill or be killed instinct flared within him, and he knew full well that the only way to walk away from a fight to the death was to be the winner.

The killer.

Randall wasn't a killer. He didn't ever *want* to be one, either. He had managed to keep his nature under wraps for thirteen years thanks to Preeti, and he didn't ever want to know what it was like to end someone's life.

What was it Ellis had said? *"If Barnes is looking for revenge..."*

Ellis had killed Jonas.

Oh, god. Suddenly it all fell into place. Jonas had come to attack Ellis, and Ellis had killed him. That was why Jonas wasn't around to ask questions of, and *that* was why Barnes wanted Ellis dead. Worse, why Barnes loathed Ellis so much.

Ellis *was* a killer.

Was that why Ellis had gone along with Randall's idea? Did he plan to find Barnes and kill him? Was Randall aiding a murder?

If he didn't, would Ellis die?

Randall was so caught up in his realisation that he almost didn't notice the fresh splash of Barnes' scent in the air.

TWENTY-TWO

ELLIS STUMBLED. Randall had stopped abruptly and now he growled, the sound sending vibrations up Ellis' arm and into his shoulder.

"Randall?" he whispered. He tightened his grip on the harness and strained to listen.

There. He heard a second heartbeat. It was quick, and accompanied by footsteps.

Randall's growl grew into a full, deep-throated snarl of warning.

"Barnes?" Ellis faced the oncoming heartbeat and tried not to let his arse-clenching dread show.

The heartbeat accelerated, and the footfalls neared. "O'Neill."

It was him. The same accent, the same voice. They were five minutes from Ellis' flat. If Ellis' mental map was correct they were on Market Mews, a deserted street with no windows, no homes. It was perfect for walking to and from the gallery without drawing attention.

It would be the perfect spot to kill a man in, too, if that was Barnes' intention.

"I don't know what you want," Ellis said. He squeezed the harness so tightly that his nails gouged into his own palm. "But we can work something out. Let's talk. Come to the office, we can have a cup of tea, and whatever it is you-"

Too many things happened at once: Randall jerked forward and twisted Ellis off-balance; Barnes' gasped and his pulse spiked; a hand closed around Ellis' right shoulder and snagged a fistful of clothing.

Ellis tried to shove against Barnes' body, and then something sharp punctured his left arm. It speared through his clothes and into his bicep, and it hurt like white hot fire.

And then he wasn't holding the harness any more.

Because he didn't have an arm any more.

He opened his mouth to scream, but he hadn't thought to take a breath to do so. He heard the surreal sound of a million grains of sand pouring out of his left sleeve.

Ash. It's ash.

What the hell could have ashed his whole arm like that?

He wasn't given the time to work it out. Barnes threw him against the shutters of a garage, which clattered in protest. Ellis sprawled against the slats of metal to try and stay upright but the failure of his missing arm to do as it was told made him tumble to the pavement in a heap.

He dimly heard Randall's snarls lower to a fearful whimper, and forced his lungs to take in air.

"Leave him alone," he begged.

"Your dog is not so stupid, eh?" Barnes leered. He kicked Ellis viciously in the stomach, and Ellis writhed onto his side to try and protect his midriff. "Even he can see you are not worth dying for."

Ellis scrabbled at the cold, cracked pavement with his right hand and tried to prop himself up to better locate Randall. He could hear the werewolf's ragged panting and erratic heartbeat, but Randall wasn't moving. Ellis didn't smell blood; it didn't seem that Randall was injured.

God damn it, wasn't the whole reason for this stupid ruse so that Randall could protect him if they encountered Barnes? Why hadn't he stepped in?

Was he going to just sit there and let Ellis die?

Ellis could feel his own body work to regenerate the injury. Resources that lay dormant were awakening and bleeding toward his shoulder, leaving cold in their wake. There was nothing he could do to stop the process, and he had no idea how long it would be before his arm was healed. He didn't exactly go around cutting his own limbs off just to find out.

"Tell me what you want," he rasped.

Barnes barked a snort, bleak laugh. "What I want, Mr. Ellis O'Neill, is to destroy you."

Ellis heard Barnes drop into a crouch, and he pressed himself back against the garage door.

"You are a leech. A parasite, in every sense of the word. You take the life of others and you use it. And then when you are done, you discard us like cattle and search for your next meal."

Ellis scowled. "I bloody well do not-"

"Silence!" Barnes' scream was like a smack to the face, and Ellis shrank away from it.

Randall growled.

"You stay, dog," Barnes snarled at Randall, "or I will do for you as I will for your master."

Ellis could only listen in horror as Randall backed down again.

"Maybe he is that stupid after all," Barnes said. He grabbed Ellis' right shoulder again and dragged him up off the floor until he sat with his back to the door.

Oh god, Ellis thought. *This is it.*

Thanks for nothing, Randall.

"Why are you doing this?" Ellis whispered. "Please. Just tell me why."

"You killed Jonas," Barnes snarled. "But it's more than that. You kill *careers*, O'Neill, and those you don't kill you just drain until there is nothing left. Art is not a commodity! It is not a thing for you to put a price on and decide who can and cannot afford to pay. Creatures like you are the death of the artist, O'Neill. You say that you love art, that you cherish it, that you yearn to bring art to the people, but it is *you* who is destroying it for everyone!"

Ellis tried to grab Barnes' arm but Barnes twisted, and all Ellis got was a fistful of coat. He clung to it, though; it gave him some measure of where exactly Barnes was.

"I don't know what you're talking about," Ellis said, attempting to inject every scrap of sincerity into his words that he could muster. "I don't know who Jonas is, and-"

Barnes slammed him back against the garage door. "I know what you did," he hissed.

"I didn't do anything! For god's sake, Barnes! I'm an art dealer! I'm not a murderer!"

"You killed him. And I will kill you. I know how to destroy your kind, leech. I am not some amateur."

As far as Ellis was aware, somehow taking all his body parts off him would probably work, and that didn't take years of research to figure out. Whatever the hell Barnes had used to lop a whole arm off at once left Ellis in no doubt that he faced a slow and painful death while Barnes gleefully sliced everything else off until there was nothing left but dust.

"How?" Ellis whimpered.

He heard a *tink* of metal against the pavement. The sound was clear and short, like a muffled bell. "I have a blade," Barnes sneered, "of true silver."

Ellis froze.

The shaft of silvery light had penetrated his heart in the painting. Jesus Christ, no wonder Ellis had lost his whole arm to a single wound. If that thing got into his heart...

Silver.

He groaned weakly. Was that why Randall was hanging back? Barnes probably thought the 'dog' understood a threat from a bladed weapon, but if Randall could see that it was silver that could well be why he hadn't jumped in.

That would mean the superstitions about werewolves and silver were true, and if that were the case he couldn't blame Randall for his reticence to get involved.

Ellis was buggered, but hopefully Randall would survive. If he kept up the dog act he could run away, and there was nothing a human being on two legs could do to catch him.

He laughed faintly. "Silver," he echoed. "I thought everyone believed it was wood."

His laugh faltered.

Everyone *did* believe it was wood, didn't they? You had to go for some serious digging to find out about silver.

Or you had to be a vampire. Which was silly. Barnes wasn't one. Ellis could hear his heart, smell his breath, feel his warmth as it seeped slowly into his shoulder.

"Fine," Ellis snarled. "Yes. I killed Jonas. Is that what you want me to say?"

"No." Barnes leaned in closer. "I want you to say *how* you killed him."

Ellis winced. "You don't. If you cared about him, you don't want to hear-"

"Tell me!"

"For god's sake! He came into my gallery and threatened my dog, so I beat him to death against the damn floor!"

"YOU LIE!" Barnes roared.

Ellis felt the tip of the knife slice a cut against his chest, and god alone knew how much of him turned to dust under its touch and cascaded down beneath his shirt. The rot hadn't reached his heart, and perhaps it hadn't even passed his ribs, but suddenly his body had two injuries to contend with.

His extremities grew colder.

His stomach roiled with hunger.

He couldn't take much more of this. Either he'd succumb to his hunger and attack Barnes, or Barnes would stab him through the heart before he could reach Barnes' blood.

"I don't understand," he whispered. "What do you think I did?"

Barnes leaned in. "I think," he said, his voice trembling with hatred, "that you fed from him until he was nothing more than dust. I think that you cannibalised him. I think that you are a vile thing who has committed the gravest sin any creature can visit upon its own kind. You consumed him, O'Neill. You drained every last drop from him, and that is how he died."

"How?" Ellis sagged as the fight drained from him. How could Barnes possibly know?

If a human being had worked it out, there was no way to stop anyone else catching on. Ellis' days were numbered. He'd destroyed Jonas in an act punishable by death and some random nutter off the damn street *knew*.

"A simple thing," Barnes hissed. "Something you gave away to me the first time that we ever spoke, and you have confirmed every time since then. Something you do even now, as you lay dying in a gutter."

Ellis shook his head. "What is it?"

Barnes laughed bitterly. "You do not even know? Idiot. We are speaking Polish."

Ellis' jaw worked. Nothing came out.

He didn't speak Polish.

TWENTY-THREE

RANDALL HAD TRIED to pull Ellis back from Barnes as the painter lunged, but it had gone horribly wrong. It was bound to. Ellis had no idea which way Randall was about to go or when he would move.

He saw the knife as though everything moved in slow motion. The blade gleamed in the moonlight in the way that only pure silver could, and after Barnes sank it into Ellis' coat Ellis' entire left arm had fallen apart. It rained down over Randall's coat and sounded like wire bristles sweeping over cymbals.

Randall circled Barnes slowly, trying to find an opening, but Barnes held the knife against Ellis' chest. Barnes seemed to be gloating, but Randall didn't understand the language.

Ellis spoke it just fine, though. He didn't hesitate, and there weren't pause sounds like he was trying to find the right word. Whatever they were conversing in Ellis was every bit as fluent as Barnes.

He thought for a second that he had an opportunity. Ellis had said something to rile Barnes, and Barnes screamed into his face, but when Randall snarled the knife was waved at him, and he had to shrink back from it.

Randall had never faced silver before. Their pack worked hard to stay under the radar and not expose their existence to the humans that surrounded them. They took their frustrations underground and they never changed shapes in the open. They didn't charge through a densely populated city wearing their wolf bodies no matter what time of day or night it was. Wolves were extinct in England and had been for over five hundred years, and nobody expected to see one in the wild. There was no mistaking any of them for a dog. The wolf's body was leaner, the legs longer, and the hackles thick with protective fur. They weren't remotely domesticated, and their eyes were golden, not brown or blue or anything else humans considered safe and reassuring.

He knew how dangerous it was, though. When they were younger, Preeti had switched out her gold earrings for a silver-plated pair. She'd barely had one earring in for five seconds before she collapsed screaming on the ground. Briar had to take it out for her to prevent her from tearing it out through her own flesh.

The knife in Barnes' hand *sang* to him. It twisted Luna's song as she bathed the world in her pure, radiant light and it turned her beauty into something lethal. Randall didn't know if it was magic or science, and he didn't care. It made no difference. Silver weapons were forbidden: Briar wanted no such dangerous things near his people, and Randall was inclined to agree. Even if they ever fell into a border skirmish with other packs, Briar wanted to ensure that silver stayed out of the fight. It was unconscionable to use the metal knowing the pain it could bring.

If wearing earrings plated with silver hurt like hell, Randall never wanted to find out what being stabbed with a blade made of it would feel like.

He hadn't thought of himself as a coward. He saw violence as unnecessary; a failure of intelligence and reason. He endured everything from playful shoves to abrupt beatings, but he'd never run from bullies, and he wasn't about to now. Ellis had told him to save himself.

Well, screw that.

Barnes screamed again, and the tip of his knife slid through Ellis' shirt, barely scratching the vampire's skin. It was enough to cause another cascade of ash.

Randall grimaced, but held his tongue. He'd seen the painting: Ellis' heart had to be Barnes' final goal, and reaching it would be no problem if silver could slice through a vampire's body so easily.

He hunkered down carefully to minimise the rustle from his

fluorescent jacket and avoid drawing Barnes' eye with the motion. Randall *had* to take Barnes' knife-arm, or Barnes would stab him with that damn blade in self-defence. He had to do it without pushing the silver any further into Ellis' body lest the rescue attempt be the very thing that killed him. And he had to take action without giving Barnes the opportunity to finish Ellis off before Randall could stop him.

So he waited.

Barnes was quieter now, smug and satisfied as Ellis' expression slackened in shock.

Barnes' muscles adjusted. His posture changed. He lifted his elbow to change the angle of the knife.

He was going to murder Ellis, right now, and Ellis couldn't even see it coming.

Randall was out of time, and the wolf in him made a decision.

He sprang and took Barnes' forearm in his teeth. His feet landed against Ellis' chest, and he immediately kicked off against the vampire to draw Barnes' blade away from his skin.

Barnes screamed. The knife fell from his hand.

The wolf tightened his jaws until he felt the resistance of bone and he dragged Barnes to the ground. The taste of blood ran freely over his tongue and mingled with Luna's bright song.

He gave himself to the music and shook his body to worry the limb trapped between his jaws until it broke in a chorus of snaps so close together they were like popping candy.

Barnes flopped and scrabbled for his knife with his left hand. Randall pushed back against the pavement and dragged Barnes out into the road, away from the blade before he could reach it.

Checkmate.

He couldn't release Barnes, or the painter would reach his knife. He couldn't stay here holding Barnes all damn night either: the man was wailing like a banshee and sooner or later someone would hear it.

Kill him.

The wolf knew how to survive. Kill or be killed. This wasn't a decision any human should have to face, but it was one the beast could make for him, and it was ready to. It *wanted* to. He could release Barnes' arm and be on his throat within seconds, and it would all be over.

He heard something over the desperate sounds Barnes made. A rasp of metal against concrete.

Darkness rose from the edge of the pavement and fell on Barnes. Randall caught a glimpse of Ellis' deathly-pale features contorted in the cold, hard rage of a predator, but his attention was drawn to the knife Ellis now held in his remaining hand.

Silver flashed in the moonlight, and Ellis drove the blade deep into Barnes' lower back.

Barnes shuddered, and his screams turned to guttural rasps.

"We have to go," Ellis snarled. "Do you understand me? We have to go!" He put a foot on Barnes' back so that he could drag the knife free, then wobbled back from the body and crouched to regain his balance.

Randall froze in horror. Ellis intended to leave Barnes in the street to bleed to death. Randall's wolf wanted to end it; tear his throat out and kill his enemy.

How was that any better than Ellis' way? At least Barnes stood a chance of calling an ambulance for himself if they left him.

And coming back to kill Ellis another night.

Ellis fumbled the knife into his jacket pocket, then moved toward Randall, reaching out with his lone hand to try and find him. Once he made contact, his hand slid along Randall's coat until he could snag the harness, and he dragged on it frantically. The predatory set was gone from his features, replaced by urgency. "Take me home. For god's sake, *move!*"

Spurred into action, Randall released Barnes' fractured arm and dragged Ellis away until Barnes' whimpers were nothing more than a memory.

TWENTY-FOUR

ELLIS STUMBLED after Randall and held the harness so tightly that if he fell Randall would have to bloody drag him across the street. He could hear Barnes behind them, his breath heavy and his heart struggling arhythmically. The smell of Barnes' blood was driving nails into Ellis' brain; he had to get away before his hunger overrode all reason.

He should have made sure Barnes was dead. Barnes knew far, far too much, but that didn't give Ellis the right to execute him; that was for the Constabulary to handle if they found a mortal with that knowledge.

The problem with pointing the Constabulary toward Barnes was that Barnes' knowledge centred around something Ellis shouldn't be able to do.

How the hell could they have been speaking Polish the entire time? Worse, how could Ellis know whether he was engaging in English if he'd somehow taken on Jonas' power?

He swore silently. How long had this been going on? Were there customers who thought Ellis was fluent in Arabic, French, and twenty Chinese dialects?

Jesus, no wonder Jonas thought it was useless. It was *dangerous*. Nobody could be fluent in every language ever spoken. How long would it be before this ability stretched the boundaries of serendipity and stepped fully over into suspicious? Was there no way to control it, or at least recognise when it was being used?

He felt his teeth with his tongue. His fangs hadn't come down, at least, but the hunger clawed at him as his body fed on its limited resources to continue its healing. When did he last feed? A week or two ago? God, it was before he'd even met Randall, that was for sure, and now he had a whole arm to re-grow, as well as whatever damage Barnes had done to his chest.

He should have fed from Barnes.

No. *No.* He'd made Randall take him away to *prevent* that. Barnes was too close to death to feed from; if he died while Ellis was still feeding, the wound wouldn't heal up properly. He'd leave a damn great bite mark that police forensics would scratch their heads over for years to come. Worse, the Constabulary would get involved regardless. A body found on a vampire's home territory with blood missing? It would draw an investigation, and Ellis didn't want the Constabulary to tie him to a messy death. Human politics were bad enough, but if Ellis' name came up twice in one year for brazen murders the mud might begin to stick, and it could stay on him for decades.

He should have anticipated an attack so close to home. Had Barnes been waiting in the Mews for him all night? No, he couldn't have; he would have jumped them both earlier. Had he expected Ellis to stay at the gallery until his more usual leaving hour, and come to lay in ambush at a time when Ellis was more likely to be on his way home from work? That seemed far more likely.

Ellis' arm was almost yanked from its socket as Randall turned a corner, and for once Ellis didn't complain. His empty sleeve fluttered uselessly against his side as they half-jogged through the winding back-streets. The night was eerily quiet, filled only with distant sounds of traffic, restaurants or bars, and Ellis gave silent thanks to Randall's forethought.

If it weren't for Randall, he'd be dead. There wasn't any doubt about that. Ellis would have stayed at the gallery late and alone, and Barnes would have been in Market Mews at the right time. Tiberius would have got himself hurt, or worse.

Ellis owed Randall his life.

God, he shouldn't have doubted the werewolf. He'd been right there the whole time, and he'd leaped in to tear Barnes off Ellis at the moment Randall had deemed to be right. Ellis had put his existence in Randall's paws and Randall hadn't let him down. Hell, with silver involved, the wolf had been in every bit as much danger as Ellis, if not more, and he'd *still* torn Barnes' body so violently that Ellis had heard bones twist and snap.

And then he'd smelled the blood.

He groaned. He'd jammed a knife into Barnes' body. What had he been thinking? Was he trying to kill Barnes? Finish him off so he couldn't talk? Or was it revenge, pure and simple? A childish tantrum, an eye for an eye, a vicious attack in retaliation for the pain Barnes had caused him?

He wasn't proud, by any means. He wasn't a violent man, yet this was the second time he'd attacked someone with the intent to kill. Was this the true curse of vampirism? Was his monstrosity not in what he was, but the actions he took to protect himself?

Randall must hate him by now. All the wolf had done was take Barnes off Ellis. He'd done it savagely, but Barnes should have survived some shattered bones and mauled flesh. Then Ellis had stuck a bloody knife into Barnes - god alone knew where. Somewhere soft and squishy. Ellis had lashed out toward Barnes' heartbeat and his warmth, and he felt the resistance against the knife as it slid into meat instead of bouncing off tarmac.

Fuck. What if Ellis had killed Barnes?

What if he hadn't?

He skidded to a halt as Randall stopped. "What? What is it?" He whispered to try and keep the panic from his voice.

"Hrrooonnhhh," Randall bristled.

Did that sound a little bit like *home*?

Fuck. Did Jonas' power mean that Ellis understood Randall's growls, or was he projecting?

"Home?"

"Rrrf." *Yes.* He already knew that sound, and it was affirmative.

Ellis lay the harness against Randall's back and nudged his jacket aside so that he could dig his wallet out of his trouser pocket. He took the doorsteps carefully, felt for the doorframe and across to the card slot, then slid his key card in and twisted the handle once the lock clicked. He shouldered the door and stepped inside. "Quick," he hissed to Randall.

Randall didn't need to be told twice. He snaked in through the door while Ellis held it, and his claws clattered on the century-old mosaic tile.

Ellis closed the door and took a moment to lean against it, then pocketed his wallet and grabbed Randall's harness. "Stairs," he whispered.

Randall trotted through the vast, echoing hallway and stopped again. Ellis let go of the harness and reached for the handrail, then nodded. "Go."

They ascended all six sets of stairs. The building was only three storeys, but Ellis' flat was the top floor and each floor was almost double the height of a modern home. His fingers slid over the polished wood that had become glassy-smooth through decades of use and varnish, and he began to feel as though he might be safe at last.

The door to his flat still used keys, not electronics, and he unlocked it the old-fashioned way. Once they were in he stopped to check every last deadbolt, latch and mortice lock in his door.

Home, at last. Still alive.

He sagged weakly against the door for a moment, but he couldn't stay there propped against it for long.

Randall was waiting.

Ellis turned and reached for the wolf, then crouched beside him and struggled to unfasten Tiberius' coat and harness one-handed. The velcro was relatively easy, and he had the coat off within moments. The plastic clips were harder to deal with, and he swore until he managed to get them to click. Ellis unbuckled the chest strap and wriggled the harness off over Randall's head, and heard Randall shake like a wet dog.

He tucked coat and harness away on the shelf made for them, and then he moved into the flat and felt the outside of his jacket pocket so that he could work out where the hilt of the knife lay and avoid removing his other hand when he dipped in to pull the weapon free. He set it well out of the way, on the mantel of the fireplace, before he crouched to fuss Tiberius.

Poor Tiberius, who was fast asleep, and whose tail swished tiredly at being woken.

"You're a good boy," Ellis whispered. "Yes, you are. Go back to sleep."

By some miracle of willpower, Ellis found his way to the couch and dropped into it, collapsing with exhaustion.

He heard the grotesque sounds of Randall changing shape, and Ellis drew a breath.

They would have to talk. Sooner or later, they'd need to talk about tonight.

"Randall," he began. "I'm so sorry-"

Randall's bare feet made little noise as the werewolf padded across the floor toward him. Ellis felt Randall's fingers roughly grab the front of his torn shirt, and he paused, bewildered.

Did Randall get the knife on his way over? No, he couldn't have; Ellis didn't smell Barnes' dried blood come any closer, but then dried blood didn't give off much of its scent until it began to decay.

After everything they'd been through, was Randall going to destroy him in his own home?

That could be for the best. Randall wasn't normal by any stretch of the imagination; he'd have the good sense to tidy up after himself and make it look like Ellis had just disappeared one night. He'd take good care of Tiberius, too; the man trained dogs with kindness. He wouldn't leave one alone to starve to death in a flat he couldn't escape.

Randall tore the glasses from Ellis' face. They thumped softly against the couch, tossed aside, and Ellis winced as light crept in. Randall's face was inches from his own, his hot breath flowing over Ellis' face, and he grabbed Ellis by the hair with his free hand.

Ellis lifted his chin, determined to meet whatever Randall had in mind with some final shred of dignity. "I'm sorry," he said again, more clearly. "I can't undo what happened any more than I can undo what I feel for you-"

This time his words were stolen, not willfully aborted. Randall's mouth was on his, kissing with savage need. The taste of iron on his tongue made Ellis writhe in Randall's grip, and when Randall straddled his lap the naked werewolf's erection pressed hard into Ellis' stomach.

"Mmphh-" He couldn't speak, couldn't get his lips away from Randall's to shape them in any meaningful way. Randall released his hair and tore at Ellis' shirt with ferocious strength. The material ripped from the cut in it, and buttons tore free from their stitches.

Randall didn't want to destroy him. Hell no. No, what Randall wanted was made abundantly clear.

How could he want this? Now? After everything Ellis had done? After all that he was?

Randall stripped him like he was a doll, and sashayed down Ellis' thighs to rip at his fly. Ellis groaned and floundered one foot against the other to kick his shoes off so that by the time Randall tore free from the kiss and began to wrench the trousers down Ellis' thighs they were out of the way.

"Randall!"

"I want you to fuck me," Randall snarled.

Ellis ached. Hunger and need and the taste of blood and the feel of Randall's short, hard body against his chest swept all his thoughts and insecurities aside.

"Better take me to the bedroom, then," he answered roughly.

Randall scooped Ellis into his arms and lifted him from the couch, and Ellis's lips found Randall's shoulder.

Just a little. That's all he needed. Just enough to heal, enough to get his arm back. Randall wouldn't miss a drop.

Fuck.

TWENTY-FIVE

RANDALL LEFT the bedroom door open. He needed to fuck, and he needed it *now*. God, he'd never been so bloody horny in his life.

This was wrong. Somehow, for some reason he couldn't pinpoint, this wasn't right. He tossed Ellis down onto the king-sized bed and didn't give the vampire time to get comfortable. Randall clambered up over his body and went in for another, desperate kiss as he rubbed himself invitingly against Ellis' stiffening cock.

Ellis' eyes were bright with lust, and he bit Randall's lip, teeth firm for a second.

"Jesus," Randall groaned. "I need you."

"There's a drawer," Ellis rasped, "by the bed."

"So?"

Ellis' lip curled. "There might be lube in it."

Randall rocked his hips and ground his cock against Ellis' stomach. "*Might* be?"

"It's not like I keep it around for years on end on the off-chance! I haven't a clue if there's still some in there!"

Randall grumbled and pushed himself upright. The light spewing in through the open door cast Ellis' white skin into stark relief, and suddenly Randall was struck by the sight of what was missing.

Ellis' chest had a cavity scooped from it the size of half an orange. The dip in his flesh was thankfully cast into shadow so that Randall couldn't see into it.

More glaring was Ellis' left shoulder. The beginnings of an arm started from the joint then just... stopped, like it had rotted off. Jagged bone protruded from meat which didn't bleed, didn't smell, and Randall could have sworn that the bone was rebuilding itself one millimetre at a time.

Ellis' chest rose as he took in air to speak. "What is it?"

"Nothing," Randall lied. The sight had managed to give him some small measure of self-control though, and he drew back from Ellis. His feet landed on the floor and he didn't take long to find the drawer and search through it with frantic sweeps of his fingers.

A grey box which said it was a clock but had no display; a spare pair of sunglasses in a case; a rolled-up packet of dog treats; a couple of handkerchiefs, neatly folded. Randall dug deeper until his fingers closed around a tube at the back of the drawer, and gripped it triumphantly when he saw what it was.

Ellis wriggled further up the bed to give Randall more space, and Randall crawled back over him without bothering to close the drawer.

"Success?" Ellis grinned.

"Yeah."

"Good. Slow down, cowboy."

Randall shook as he slid his crease along the length of Ellis' shaft. He whined, a wordless request.

Ellis' cold fingers slipped down Randall's side, stroking him, soothing him. "Shh. Randall. We'll get there. I promise, we'll get there. Kiss me."

He fell forward and did as he was told, and Ellis' arm snaked around him to hold him still.

Ellis moved his hips slowly, teasing Randall's crease with his length and sending a flurry of shudders through his body. Ellis' tongue invaded his mouth and took it over, tongue pushing in slowly at first, encouraging Randall to suck on it until he felt pinned between tongue and cock.

Randall drew Ellis' tongue in further and tipped his head to the side so that he could suckle for all he was worth. Every thrust of Ellis' hips squeezed Randall's meat between their stomachs, and he began to leak from his tip, slicking their skin with his desire.

"Shh," Ellis withdrew his tongue. His fingers began to stroke lightly down Randall's spine. "Relax. We've all the time in the world."

Randall drew a deep, trembling breath and released it slowly. The motion cleared his head slightly, and he managed to focus on Ellis' face.

"Better," Ellis whispered. "I don't want to hurt you, petal."

"I'd heal," Randall insisted.

"That's not the point." Ellis brushed his cold lips across Randall's jaw, and his stubble scratched faintly over Randall's skin. "But I'll bear it in mind." He rubbed his cheek down the side of Randall's neck until his lips nestled against the soft skin at the side of his throat, where he let out a desperate, yearning groan.

Randall convulsed. Ellis' touch, his sounds, reached deep into his lust and tugged on it, bending it to his will. How did Ellis *do* this to him? How had a few words and a light touch calmed Randall back to a less frenzied, more controlled state? Randall had been consumed with yearning, willing to take Ellis' cock into himself dry and suffer the consequences just to have Ellis fuck him at last and Ellis had drawn him back from that precipice. Sure he was gently nudging Randall back toward it again, but at a gentler pace; one they could both handle.

Ellis' teeth scraped across his throat, and Randall caught his breath. Ellis' icy tongue ran slowly up toward Randall's ear, and he kissed his way back down to bite again, more firmly.

Cold. Ellis wasn't cool to the touch, he was unmistakably cold.

What did that mean?

Ellis didn't let him dwell on it. He took Randall's lips with his own and kissed him fervently, his mouth becoming voracious, demanding. He took his hand from Randall's spine and insinuated it between their undulating bodies and, once he found Randall's cock, his fingers closed around it and squeezed; gently at first, giving Randall time to move and accommodate his hand, and then with a tighter grip.

Randall sagged against Ellis' body, delirious, driven almost mad with longing.

"Please," he whispered.

Ellis moved his hand, stroking Randall's shaft in slow motion. His lips found their way to Randall's throat again, as though guided by pure instinct, and he lapped and nuzzled, scraped and bit. His groans grew in their insistence with every return of his mouth to Randall's tender flesh.

They moved together in squirming, rippling unison, and an eerie sense of calm, relaxed bliss settled into Randall's core.

He was *safe*. Ellis was taking care of him, chasing away the full moon and replacing it with pure, delicate care.

"Ready?" Ellis breathed against his ear.

"Fuck, yes," Randall answered.

"Good. Go on." His hand slowed to a stop.

Randall's skin prickled in anticipation, but he was able to sit up and open the lube without much effort. He squirted it into his hands and rubbed them together, then reached behind himself and worked both hands up Ellis' length, one after the other, coating him in it.

Ellis' head fell back and his back arched lightly. He barely made a sound, but his grip on Randall's cock twitched and squeezed.

Randall gripped Ellis around the base, and nudged himself backward, seeking Ellis' tip with his sphincter.

"Slowly," Ellis hissed. His hand lifted from Randall's shaft and he touched Randall's chest instead, then moved his hand up further to settle around Randall's throat. His head and shoulders lifted from the sheets so that he could reach, and while his grip was gentle, it was possessive as all hell.

Randall licked his lips and nodded obediently.

"Breathe," Ellis reminded him.

He sucked in air and released it slowly. Then again, until he fell back into that blissful near-trance he felt under Ellis' touch.

Then he lowered himself, one breath at a time, onto Ellis' cock until it was buried deep inside him.

"Jesus," Ellis sighed. "I love you."

Randall stirred from his cloud and gazed down at Ellis. For some reason he couldn't think of what to say.

Ellis laughed softly. "Kiss me again, you beautiful creature."

Randall leaned forward, and Ellis gently lifted his knees to keep himself deep inside him. When their lips met, Ellis released his throat and slid his arm around Randall's waist to hold him close.

"Did you mean that?" Randall finally asked.

"That you're beautiful?"

"That you love me."

Ellis grinned crookedly. "Aye."

Randall's head spun, and he tilted it aside, lifting his jaw so that he could press his throat against Ellis' lips. "Do it," he whimpered, voice raw.

Ellis' arm tensed, and his hips lifted slightly, pushing a rasp out of Randall's lungs. His teeth grazed across Randall's skin, and he groaned "Randall-"

"You need it," Randall said. It hit him like a minor epiphany. "That's why you're so cold. You need it, don't you? You're hurt. God, Ellis, if you need it, *take* it."

Ellis bit into Randall's flesh. It wasn't hard; it didn't hurt. He seemed to be stuck there, doing nothing, saying nothing.

"Christ, you trusted me with your *life*," Randall whimpered. "Now I'm trusting you with mine. For god's sake, do it!"

He felt a sharp stab into his skin. It scratched like a needle, and he gulped down a fleeting glimmer of fear before his body became suffused with raw, paralysing pleasure. It rolled through him like an orgasm and his body ceased to be under his own control. Just like that, Ellis had him, and he couldn't do a damn thing to resist if he'd wanted to.

He didn't want to.

Ellis' hips ground against his rear and drove his cock deep into Randall's insides, and Randall's breath came shallow, fast. His pulse rushed in his ears; he lay immobile, gasping, as Ellis drove into him.

He wanted to cry out, to howl, to scream his pleasure so loud the neighbours complained, but he couldn't utter a sound, couldn't so much as lift a finger. He felt Ellis tighten under him, and his own climax dragged nearer, but he was utterly at the mercy of Ellis' bite.

When he came, it was explosive. It ripped through him and shredded his thoughts. His insides pulsed and grasped hungrily at Ellis, and his balls squeezed tight. He let out a strangled howl which ballooned a hundredfold as Ellis' fangs withdrew from his body.

By the time he was done, he was a wreck. Boneless, he felt like he'd melted over Ellis' body and would stay stuck there forever.

Ellis' lips were warm as they tenderly kissed his jaw.

I love you, Randall desperately wanted to say, but he couldn't find the strength, so he just lay with Ellis and let the aftershocks wrack his body.

TWENTY-SIX

IT WASN'T until they made it into the bathroom together and turned the light on that Randall saw Ellis in full, and the change in him was a shock.

The wound in his chest was gone.

His arm had fully regrown.

His skin was flush, pink with life and vitality.

"Shit," he stammered.

Ellis laughed. "Five out of ten for effort, but if you're going to slap a pet name on me could you make it something a bit more flattering?"

"You're-" Randall shook his head slowly. There was *no* not-dumb way to say *you've got your arm back* that he could think of. "Um, I mean, you…"

"It's all right." Ellis stretched out his left hand. He seemed to understand what had thrown Randall for a loop, and looked mildly perplexed himself. "I know what you mean."

"Is that, er. Is it normal?"

"I don't make a habit of letting my arms drop off, but-" Ellis shook his head. "I've had a few bumps and scrapes. If I've fed, they patch up pretty quick, but this is…" He trailed off and flexed his arm, as though he were trying on a new coat. "I expected it to take longer. It's your blood, I think. It's ambrosia, no two ways about it; I haven't felt so alive in-" He sucked his teeth, then ran his tongue over them. "Well, I've *never* felt this alive, even when I was."

"You're not actually dead," Randall snorted.

"I dunno. It's all semantics really. I don't think concepts like alive or dead really take this precise circumstance into consideration." Ellis reached for Randall until he found the shifter's arm, then hooked a hand around his elbow. "Shower?"

Randall's head bobbed and he led Ellis toward the glass at the end of the bathroom. "I heal like there's no tomorrow," he admitted as he reached for the dial and started the shower. Warm water rained down on them a few moments before it picked up some more heat. "Maybe you picked up some of that-" *from my blood.*

Randall swallowed. There wasn't any doubting how it had felt, but that's what Ellis had done, wasn't it? Fed from him?

Ellis smiled a little, but it looked sad. "Randall?"

"Yeah. I'm okay. Sorry, it's all just-"

"A bit much?"

Randall nodded. "Yeah."

Ellis' smile relaxed. He reached for the shower gel and began to lavish attention across Randall's chest, his fingers slippery with lather as they explored and cleansed in equal measure. "Are you happy?"

"Wow." Randall gazed up at him, trying to work out what he meant by that. "Like, right now?"

"In life. I won't pry, but I am running with the assumption that you aren't the only werewolf in town?"

Randall bit his lip. "That's a safe bet to make."

"And you know that I'm not the only vampire in London. So while I can't begin to know what your life is like, I'll at least 'appen as you don't exist in a vacuum?"

Randall chuckled. "Also true."

Ellis' lips quirked with that little half-smirk, half-smile he had. "My life is okay. I run a business, I keep busy, but I don't *live*. I exist. I coast from night to night and it's a constant struggle just to pay the rent. There's no joy in being undead, and there's sure as hell no fun in being blind." His hands stilled and his brows furrowed in concentration. Randall saw his pupils contract faintly as Ellis made a concerted effort to focus on his features. "But there's joy in being with you. Two weeks ago I wouldn't have given a damn if Barnes had succeeded, but now?" He grit his teeth and leaned forward an inch. "I don't know what I am to you, but to me you are a reason to *be*. You're something good, something pure, and you're worth fighting to stay afloat for."

Randall squirted gel into his palms and rubbed them together. At first he focused on washing the remaining lube from his skin, but then he lathered up a fresh dollop of gel and began to wash Ellis' chest.

Everything Ellis was should have been wrong, but then everything about Randall suggested he should be a monster. It could be about time that Randall re-evaluated his ideas about the differences between monsters and men. Barnes wasn't anything he's think of as supernatural, but there was no way Randall could deny that the artist was monstrous. What kind of man set out to terrorise his target? He'd looked set on inflicting some suffering before he went in for the kill, too: Randall didn't doubt that if Barnes hadn't taken Ellis' arm by accident, he would've begun cutting pieces off deliberately. He had an axe to grind, words to say, and he would've wanted the time to say whatever it was that had made Ellis look so ill.

He swallowed, then said "What language were you two speaking?"

There it was. Straight away. The tinge of sickness flickered across Ellis' features and Randall immediately regretted his words. Fuck, why couldn't he bloody tell Ellis how he felt? Why did he have to go and ruin something beautiful?

"Polish," Ellis said. His gaze relaxed and he turned away to reach for the shampoo. He didn't turn back again. "I can't expect this of you, but I need you to make a promise to me."

"What is it?"

Ellis swept shampoo through his hair and rubbed his scalp with his fingertips. The stuff formed a white foam which smelled of wood and spices, and Ellis waited until he'd rinsed it out again before he spoke. "I need to know that you won't tell anyone I can speak or understand anything other than English. Please." He tipped his head toward Randall at last, and Randall felt his heart clench at the look of fear in Ellis' eyes. "Don't ask me why. I haven't got that figured out myself yet. But please, if you care about me in the slightest, this *has* to stay between us. Not even Jay can know. Please, promise me."

"I promise." The words left him without a second thought, and Randall hesitated before he said more firmly "I promise. Ellis, I'm sorry. I'm really shit with... with words, and people, and... who and what I am. I got bullied at school for being gay, short, black, you name it, and then when I joined a pack I got bullied there for being quiet, placid, probably short too. Whenever I go out on the scene I get objectified, fetishised, and none of it's for *who* I am. You want to know why I train dogs?"

Ellis tipped his head toward Randall.

"They don't care. They don't care about sexuality or colour or size or whether you're polite or rude or if you like pop instead of metal. They don't care about the size of your cock, the colour of your eyes, the length of your hair, or whether you bloody douched your arse before you went out. They care about structure. They care about survival and happiness and that is pretty much *it*. They're smart, and they don't judge you for the way you look; they care about what you do." Randall gripped Ellis' arms. "I do more than care about you. I'm just... I'm really not very good at-"

Ellis chuckled, then laughed weakly. "It's okay. Oh, god, it's fine. Better than fine." He sobered and leaned in to kiss Randall, slow and tender, and Randall's muscles felt about ready to turn to jelly. "This week's not been great for dates, has it? Shall we try again?"

Randall laughed with relief. "Yeah. Yeah, that'd be nice." He coughed. "Better than nice. Um, you know what I mean."

"I do, aye."

They held each other until the water began to lose its heat, and then wrapped up in towels and went back to the bedroom.

"Stay the night?" Ellis offered.

"I did say I'd stay by your side." Randall grinned slowly.

"I know, but even if Barnes has survived he won't come back tonight. Or any time soon. You don't have to-"

"I want to."

Ellis nodded. "Then I better show you how to unlock the door for when you want to head out."

"What makes you think I'll want to leave?"

Ellis laughed. "All I've got in is dog food."

Randall lifted his eyebrows, then burst out laughing.

EPILOGUE

ELLIS SAT IN HIS OFFICE. Jay was back from Paris; he and Han had a great time. Randall was over every night, so Ellis had given him his spare keycard and keys. Ellis had asked Jay to destroy the knife, and Jay found the blade ridiculously easy to bend before he sold the twisted lump of precious metal on to some website for a few bob.

There were no more death threats. Barnes' painting got hacked to pieces, burned, then scattered into the Thames; Randall had done that for him, and seemed glad to do so.

Randall. There was a complicated man if ever Ellis had met one. Gentle and patient, yet capable of such depth of passion that it had stolen Ellis' heart in record time. Love at first touch, perhaps? Ellis' world was art, he could readily believe in such flights of fancy. There was no doubt about the dull ache he felt whenever Randall wasn't around: when he had to work, or speak with his pack. And Ellis couldn't begin to question the fact that in Randall's absence all he did was sit around thinking about him, waiting for him, exchanging text messages or drumming his fingers on his desk impatiently.

He wasn't whole without Randall at his side. Every sound his phone made brought hope, and whenever the message or email was from Randall that hope flourished into joy.

"Good evening! Welcome to the O'Neill Gallery. How can I help you?"

Jay's voice came from downstairs. Ellis jerked upright in his chair and concentrated, but there were only two heartbeats in the building: Jay and Tiberius.

There was a vampire in his territory.

Ellis half-rose from his chair.

"No, thanks." The voice was strong, male, with an East End accent and total lack of interest in Jay. "I'm 'ere to see O'Neill."

"Oh? Do you have an appointment?"

Ellis lowered into his seat again. Jay was safe. The vampire wasn't here to attack.

He was a Constable. The same Constable who had questioned him over Jonas' death.

Fuck.

"Nope. But that's okay. I'm not a customer. I'm a friend."

"Oh. Oh, all right." Jay sounded unsure. "Do you know where you're going?"

"Oh yeah. Can't miss it."

Footsteps on the stairs. No pulse came closer.

Ellis straightened in his chair and texted Jay: *It's all right. I know him.*

The Constable rapped on the open door.

"Come in."

"Cheers." He stepped inside and closed the door after himself. "Sorry to bug you unannounced. I don't know if you remember me-" He left the half-sentence hanging, a faint uplift at the end of it.

"Constable Hughes," Ellis said. "Official business?"

"Yeah. I'm afraid so."

Ellis nodded and gestured toward the chairs facing his desk. "Then by all means, have a sit down."

Hughes walked across the room and settled into a chair. Ellis gave silent thanks to Hughes' jeans; the rasp of denim as he walked helped him pinpoint the older vampire. "It's probably nothing," Hughes said once he'd sat down. "I like to get stuff squared away, that's all."

Ellis lifted his chin and waited. Hughes liked to give people spaces to fill, and Ellis had almost fallen for it before. Not this time.

"About a week ago, some bloke died on your patch," Hughes began. "Does the name Tomasz Jasiński ring any bells with you?"

Ellis frowned. "No. Never-" He halted. "Wait. Jasiński. I read something once. He's an artist. Acrylics, I think?"

Little pieces fell into place. There was no Peter Barnes. No wonder Ellis hadn't ever heard of "Peter Barnes".

But he'd heard of Tomasz Jasiński, because Jonas had talked about him. Some artist Jonas had met, produced great paintings, Ellis should feature him in the gallery... Ellis declined, not on the merits or weaknesses of Jasiński's work, but because it felt like nepotism. He had no idea what Jasiński was to Jonas, but Jonas dropped the subject as quickly as he dropped everything else in his life.

"Was an artist. Turned up dead a few streets from here. Last I heard, all of Mayfair's yours, right?"

Ellis nodded numbly. "I don't understand. Why are you involved?"

"Eh, passes the time." Hughes sniffed, then added "Nah, seriously? No evidence of any of us lot involved, but it *is* weird. See, he got stabbed in the back, which is ultimately what killed him, but before that his right arm got totally wrecked. Radial fractures in both bones, teeth marks all over it, meat torn right off. It's like he got savaged by a dog."

Hughes' hint wasn't lost on Ellis. "Constable, Tiberius is a guide dog. They're rigorously chosen for their calm natures, ability to learn skills, and their patience. They don't attack. He wouldn't harm a bloody fly, and he *didn't*! He's never away from my side-" Christ, if anyone told the police Tiberius was a crazed killer dog they'd just put him down, no questions asked.

"O'Neill." Hughes sounded surprised. "Chill out."

Ellis bit the inside of his cheek. "Sorry. God, Aaron, I swear to you he didn't do it."

Hughes sighed. "Oh well. Mystery remains unsolved, then. Still, if they ever find the murder weapon, can I ask you to check it out?"

Ellis grimaced. "It wouldn't be my idea of fun, but if you're sure this is relevant to the Council, of course I'll help."

"Not sure."

Hughes had to be hiding something. He couldn't claim he was crossing territory on official business if there were no actual official business. The Constable suspected vampire involvement somehow, somewhere.

"What makes you think it might be?" Ellis murmured.

"It's just a hunch," Aaron said. "The post-mortem on Jasiński found residue of pure silver in the knife wound. It's a shitty weapon to kill people with; silver bends stupidly easily if it's not alloyed with something. But it's a *great* weapon to kill vampires with. It'd go through us like a hot knife through butter. Hell, it's probably just knife-shaped for the hell of it. People used to go for the good old-fashioned stake, back before wood became trendy."

"Trendy?" Ellis snorted.

"Cheap and easy, then." He heard Aaron move in the chair. "And if you don't know what to do once you've put wood in someone's heart it *looks* like you've already done the job. Anyway, my theory was that Jasiński came at you with a knife, your dog took him down in defence, and that would've been the end of it."

Ellis cursed inwardly. If Hughes had bothered to present him with this get-out story, he would have leaped at the chance.

Hughes was too damn smart.

"I'm sorry."

"Yeah. Me too. Anyway, thanks for your time. Sorry to bug you."

"It's no trouble. Let me know if you need my help."

"Will do."

Ellis offered his hand across the desk and Hughes shook it, then the Constable bid him farewell and left.

He waited until he was certain Hughes was long gone before he sent Randall a text.

I need you.

Randall's answer brought a smile to his lips, and helped to quash the dread of Hughes' visit.

I need you too.

Close enough, he sent. *Come home.*

Tooth & Claw continues in Blood Moon Rising.

TOOTH & CLAW

Visit http://ameliafaulkner.com to discover more about the characters and world of Tooth & Claw, and to sign up to Amelia's newsletter.

INHERITANCE

Laurence Riley has too many problems, and his uncontrolled psychic powers are just the tip of the iceberg. But when he accidentally summons a god, his only hope for survival might be another wild talent: the enigmatic and aloof British earl, Quentin d'Arcy.

Lose yourself in a world like no other in this award-winning series.

ACKNOWLEDGMENTS

Blind Man's Wolf is my first novel, and as such will always hold a special place in my heart. There are so many people it couldn't have happened without, and they all know who they are.

Thank you, too, for reading this far, but I'm afraid this isn't a Marvel film. There's no extra scene hidden here at the back of the book. Gold star for checking, though!

If you'd like to get sneak peeks of upcoming releases, why not join my Facebook group? You can find it here:

https://www.facebook.com/groups/ameliafaulkner/

Love,

Amelia Faulkner, London UK, June 2018.

ABOUT THE AUTHOR

Amelia Faulkner was born in Thame, Oxfordshire, and sprouted upward in short order. The ground around Thame is reasonably mucky, especially in the winter, and she can't be blamed for wanting to get away from it.

Raised on a steady diet of Star Trek and Doctor Who, Amelia stood no chance in not becoming a grade-A geek. She has sat on the board of the British Fantasy Society, contributed fiction and fluff to various published roleplaying games, and written non-fiction for SciFiNow and SFX Magazines. For every positive there is an equal and opposite negative, and Amelia is forced to admit that she loves Wild Wild West.

In her spare time she enjoys travel, photography, walking her Corgi, and trying to convince her friends to replay the Pathfinder Adventure Card Game with all the Goblins decks.

www.ameliafaulkner.com